NeW
Fiction

of Fly
By Night
xx

THE CHILL FACTOR

Edited by

Heather Killingray

First published in Great Britain in 2001 by
NEW FICTION
Remus House,
Coltsfoot Drive,
Peterborough, PE2 9JX
Telephone (01733) 898101
Fax (01733) 313524

SB ISBN 1 85929 032 9

FOREWORD

When 'New Fiction' ceased publishing there was much wailing and gnashing of teeth, the showcase for the short story had offered an opportunity for practitioners of the craft to demonstrate their talent.

Phoenix-like from the ashes. 'New Fiction' has risen with the sole purpose of bringing forth new and exciting short stories from new and exciting writers.

The art of the short story writer has been practised from ancient days, with many gifted writers producing small, but hauntingly memorable stories that linger in the imagination.

I believe this selection of stories will leave echoes in your mind for many days. Read on and enjoy the pleasure of that most perfect form of literature, the short story.

Parvus Est Bellus.

CONTENTS

TWO TONGUES IN THE SAME MOUTH
J S Dodds

It was nearly a month after she'd gone before the greeting started. And then he couldn't seem to stop. It was some sort of delayed shock, perhaps.
Everything was always late with them:

I'm late, she warned him once.

Me?

He's been snipped, she said.

Nothing came of it. And now he has nothing left - not even a photograph. They never could give each other presents, so he'd buy her flowers, instead - then find they'd perished between visits to the rented flat.

I wish I could take something wi' me which smells o' you she'd say, as they clung to each other, bracing themselves for the return of their everyday lives.

But they were in complete agreement from the off: no pictures, no tokens or momentoes; nothing in writing, ever. They only used the mobiles, and never called at home. Whatever happened, they'd bottle it out - that's what they decided - a flat denial until they were blue in the face:

We're like secret agents he joked. *They can take us to separate rooms and tell us the game's up, the other one's confessed - but we'll know it's just a bluff.*

Aye, an' if you ever tell her, I'll deny it. You'll see - I'd call you a lying bastard to your face - an' worse, she assured him gamely, pressing herself up close - *I'd damn you as a liar - or jus' a bloody fantasist.*

Waiting at the lights, his shoulders hunch. He's shaken with great dry sobs. His head sinks towards the wheel, so that he misses the green and there's a chorus of horns from behind. Alone in the car, a lift, the office, he'd be overcome, just the same way, in those first heady months after it began. But in those days, it had been a sort of delirious disbelief:

Christsake, Karen! he'd say to himself, wonderingly - astonished at the way his world had been suddenly turned upside down.

Perhaps they'd been lying to themselves for years, Neil and Karen, the old friends. And when they discovered the truth, they started lying to everyone else.

They were always late. It took so long to realise what was going on between them.

Why did you never say? she asked, soon after it began.

Why do you think? he countered; *I was afeart I'd put you off and lose what we did have.*

Same here, she said.

The timing was bad and that was that; because by the time they did find out, they were ten years too late. They had other partners, children, parents-in-law, mortgages: the whole carry-on you gather around yourself by the time you're pushing forty.

They didn't have each other - but they soon set that to rights.

The first step along the path is tentative: a friendly drink after work, an evening turning chilly. Neither of them wants to go inside the smoky bar, so Neil offers her his fleece to wear. And it's too big of course - just her thin bare legs underneath and her pretty features framed by the collar. Suddenly Neil feels he's seeing her for the first time. He finds she's beautiful. He wasn't blind - he already knew he was nursing an obscure, secret pleasure - just watching her putting it on. But all at once he's engulfed by a new and uncertain feeling. They never did give it a name.

Neil has been out of town on business for a while. After a drink or two, he blurts out his confession:

I find myself thinking of you, Karen, he tells her, *I think about you a lot - when I'm away. Don't get me wrong - I care an awful lot for Aileen. We're . . . a good team. An' I love to see the bairns again. But it's you, I'm thinking of, it's you I miss the most.*

An' I miss you, she says.

The way she's looking at him helps him carry on:

Well, do friends do that? he asks her. *I mean, do they think about each other all the time? Is that how friendship works - it makes you miserable and upset, when you're apart?*

Search me, Neil.

This is a very pleasing proposal.

There was always a chaste peck, or a friendly hug, when their homeward routes diverged. But tonight the gulf between her cheek and lips seems to be almost no distance at all - they cross it in a breath.

After a moment, each relinquishes the other awkwardly:

Sorry! they both say at the same time.

Don't be upset - it's nothing. He shivers. *Just a wee kiss and a cuddle, after all,* he says, as he walks her the rest of the way home. *It's no sae bad,* he adds; *it's no as if we've had our tongues down one another's throats!*

Perhaps it was a wish - or an invitation - because before they part, she pulls him into a doorway. Straddling his right thigh, she pushes her warm tongue into his mouth. And they've taken another step.

God, I'm sorry, Neil, she says. *You'll think I'm going to be Trouble. You'll think I'm a bunny boiler.*

A what?

You ken that film Fatal Attraction? *Glenn Close boils the bairns' bunny.*

Oh.

And they laugh - because it's funny, because they're not like that at all.

No, but it's okay, she says, *I won't be Trouble. We'll be awful cool about it, eh - the pair of us? We'll just carry on being friends.*

Do friends do this? he whispers, hopeful.

Yes, sometimes, she sighs; *oh aye, I think . . . sometimes they must.*

And each step is easier than the last:

This is easier than I thought, she tells him.

She doesn't mean the hours they've stolen from their lives to lie behind the curtains on these hushed afternoons; that's not easy at all. She means the languid ease with which she's raising a thigh to draw him tighter in.

I just dinae think . . . she sighs; *after all these years, I didnae think our bodies would make sae good a fit.*

But marriage, they find, has prepared them very well for this. They're used to the compromises every couple makes. They're practised in the giving and receiving of endearments:

I think you must be what they call a dab hand, Karen, he compliments her, bestowing a lingering kiss.

An' you're a first-class kisser, she whispers, *you really are. I dinnae know how I managed without this.*

They already know when to speak and when to listen; they're used to the judging of another's mood. And all those secret things - all those wee tricks of how to please, gleaned over the years in their marriages - now they're an unexpected bouquet, from which the lovers can slowly pluck each bloom:

You like that? he asks.

Hold still, she says; *I want to try something with you . . .*

As their mouths part, he laughs at a stray thought. It's a lover's laugh - a throaty chuckle, dissolving in the soft hollow between her shoulder and her neck.

My Nan used to say: 'Don't keep two tongues in the same mouth.' I'm no sure this is what she meant.

No, not yours and mine, surely. This canny be wrong. She kisses him again. *It feels so right; it's heaven to me,* she sighs.

It's brought him to some other place, all the same.

They were almost innocent.

I've never done this before, he volunteers.

Me neither, she tells him.

But they weren't entirely green. They've both seen the messy ways friends and colleagues conduct their affairs; the broken marriages, the upset bairns and confused, angry teenagers. It's not for them:

You're a good man, Neil. I couldn't do this, she says: *not if I wasn't sure I could count on you completely.*

And I trust you, he tells her. *You're a very sensible woman, Karen - I know you are.*
It's madness, but.

Oh aye.

An' it'll end in tears.

Aye, I know. But only ours, he says; *only ours, if we're careful.*

And careful is what they are. They need good heads on their shoulders for this game. Adultery turns spouses into children. Neil and Karen are the only grown-ups now - the ones who know what's really going on. Together, they need to plan for everyone: secretly ordering the lives of the two households, co-ordinating holidays, managing the ups and downs of their marriages, the house moves and promotions; following the progress of each other's children through school and into adolescence. And that's how Neil always imagined them - going on like this for years and years . . .

They were often late, both of them - it was so hard to get away sometimes. But one afternoon she didn't turn up at all.

Two streets from home he pulls the car over and starts to greet again.

Neil can't take an interest in anything, these days. His wife opens the post.

Well, this must be a mistake, she says; *there's a hundred pound bill on the card from some florist!*

Flowers, he tells her, matter-of-fact as he can. *A wreath, that was, for Karen.*

He never could buy her anything before.

A hundred pounds, Neil! Did they no have a wee spray or something!

For God's sake, Aileen, she was . . . she was one of our oldest friends.

One of your oldest friends, Neil, no mine. I dinnae want to speak ill . . . but I didnae like the way she looked at you sometimes. There was jus' . . . . something - I could see it in her eyes.

He turns on her. He sounds as if he's on the brink of tears:

Well, you won't have to see it now, will you? he cries. *And I'll never see it either. I'll never see that look in her eyes again.*

There's a strange silence for a while.

Oh my God, he wife says, at last. She doesn't shout back at him. In a quiet sort of voice she says: *I've jus' realised something.*

Sorry, Aileen. I'm upset. We were aye close, you know.

You loved her, she tells him.

In a way - I suppose I did.

No, she corrects him. *No. I mean, you were in love . . . All those things I couldn't quite understand, all those wee signs over the years - I saw them, but I ignored them all. Fool that I was, I trusted you.*

Neil is too full of his own grief to feel pity for his wife.

What things? he sneers. *What wee signs?*

My God, you were careful, but - the pair of you - like a couple of spies.

Don't be daft, Aileen.

And when exactly were you planning to tell me - me and that other poor sod, Iain - when all the kids had left home? Is that it . . . ?

Christ! she continues, *You're like a man wi two tongues in his head, you are. You've been a spy in my own home, my own bed. Have you ever exchanged an unguarded word wi' me, Neil Thomson, eh? All the time you were here wi' me - how many years? - That was jus' a lie. You're the beginning and end of all liars, you are. The damned pair of you have made my entire life a lie . . . God damn you, Neil!*

But Neil doesn't hang his head. He looks up at her, looks her in the eye:

But am I really such a damned liar? he asks; *or jus' a damned fantasist?*

THE TRUNK
Christine Williams

They sat back on their heels and surveyed the trunk. It was an old travelling trunk with a domed lid, covered in leather with a lock centre front.

'How could the last people forget to take something this large with them?' asked Sue.

'Well maybe they didn't want it anymore and it's quite large to carry down the steps.' Darren stood up and looked around the beams in the attic. 'I can't find a key anywhere so we'll have to break into it.'

'We can't do that,' Sue rested her hand on the trunk, then pulled it away sharply and dusted her hand on her jeans, 'it doesn't belong to us.'

'Well, the estate agent said the house had been empty for some time so I don't think anyone's going to come and claim it.'

Darren picked up a screwdriver and tried to prise the lock open. The screwdriver snapped and he grazed his knuckles on the lock. 'Ouch, bloody lock, it doesn't look that strong,' he sucked his knuckles.

'We don't need to open it, let's just get it out and get the refuse to collect it,' Sue stepped back towards the trapdoor as she spoke, the trunk looked on.

'Well if we open it we can throw away any rubbish and use it for storage, who knows it may be hiding some treasure,' Darren was giving the lock a good-looking at. 'What if I try picking it?'

'Darren I don't think you'll be able to.'

'Yes I will, I'll go and get some wire or something, I've seen it done on the telly.'

'Darren, that's not real, anyway I don't like it, I think we should throw it.'

'What's there not to like?' he laughed. 'It's an old trunk and it's a good storage container, anyway it's too heavy for us to get down.'

'What if I get my brother to come round and give us a hand, we'll shift it then.' She was pleading now.

'Let me try to open it first and then we'll see, I'll be back in a minute.'

'Don't leave me up here.' Panic was in her voice now and she grabbed his arm as he went past her.

He patted her hand, 'Don't be so daft, you're not frightened of an attic, I won't be long,' and with that he disappeared through the trapdoor and down the ladder.

Sue stayed near the door and watched the trunk; it stood and watched back. She couldn't quite decide what she didn't like about it, it looked menacing, yet it had no features to look menacing with.

'Here we are,' Darren's head popped through the trapdoor followed by his body and what looked like half his workshop, 'Something here will open it.'

Sue surveyed the tools. He had fetched a hammer and bar, a drill, plus a piece of bent wire.

'Right, I'll try to pick it first,' he knelt on one knee in front of the trunk.

'Be careful.' Sue moved to stand behind him. She watched as he poked the wire into the lock and twiddled it. 'Nothing's happening.'

'I thought this might have worked,' Darren was twisting his tongue at the side of his mouth, it was something he did when he was concentrating.

'Look, it's not working, let's leave it for now and go back to decorating the bathroom' Sue hoped he would agree.

'No, it's working, just try to slide the catch when I tell you.'

Sue placed her fingers on the catch and waited for his word.

'Now.'

She tried to move the catch down and then sideways, the wire slipped from the hole and sliced across her finger.

'Ow, that was a stupid thing to do,' she half-shouted, half-cried, 'just leave it will you?' She shook her hand and sucked her finger alternately.

'I'm sorry, are you alright baby? Let me have a look.' Darren took her hand and kissed her finger better.

'Let's just leave it please.' She looked at him pleadingly.

He turned back to the trunk, 'I'm going to use the hammer and bar, it'll make a mess of the lock but we won't ever want to lock it again, I won't be long.' Darren picked up the hammer and placed the edge of the bar against the lock. He struck the top of the bar sharply. Nothing happened. He struck it again a little harder, still nothing. 'Right,' he said. 'I'll get it this time.' He swung the hammer, it struck the bar and slid down onto his hand.

He took a sharp intake of breath as he dropped the bar and the colour drained from his face. It was the sort of pain that was so severe it took a while to register.

'Darren,' Sue screamed, 'you're an idiot, let me take a look.' She dropped to her knees by the side of the trunk facing him. He had stuck his hand between his thighs and was rocking on his knees. 'That's it, no more trying to open it, it's going out to the refuse men and I don't care how we get it out of here.'

Darren and Sue looked sharply at the trunk. The lock had sprung open and the lid was rising. They looked to see what was in it but it looked empty.

Together they leant forward to look into the bottom of the trunk and it made a sound very like a swallowing noise. Then the lid closed silently on them and the lock clicked back into place.

The trunk settled down to wait, all alone in the attic of a house that hadn't been lived in for many years.

AT NUMBER 63
Alfa

Please come straightaway
the woman from the Nursing Home said.
A relapse. She's asking for you.

Didn't expect it at all. She seemed fine last Wednesday. It was the day
when she told me I would be very rich soon.

Twenty-five is your lucky number
she said. We laughed about it. Had a lovely afternoon together. Mind
you, she did look frail, much too thin.

Hope she is alright. Should be. Always been a strong woman. Used to
go away to sea, she did. Never married. her fiance was killed. An
accident. A week before their wedding, she told me. A private person,
her. Too private for a nursing home really. Wish that nephew of hers
and his wife would take her in again. Especially now, when she needs
them more than ever. I can't take her in, can I, with him there. She
adores their little girl.

Like my dear sister, Rose
she tells me
especially the hair.

Lots of baby photos on her dressing table.
Was so pleased when the nephew married a nurse. Usually nurses are
caring people, aren't they? Not this one though. Selfish, calculating and
a snob. It was alright to move in next door when she became pregnant,
oh yes. Nowhere else to go, was there? Soon forgot the old lady's
generosity, didn't she? She took advantage instead. Both of them used
her, that precious nephew and her, that so-called nurse. All of a sudden
the area wasn't good enough for them anymore now that he is a teacher
in a private school.

Forgotten, who made it possible for him to study. He would have ended
up in a children's home, only for her.

As long as I'm alive, your boy will be alright

she had promised her sister. Must have been very close, those two. She did without many things, I know. That nephew of hers had the very best. Maybe she spoilt him. Wish somebody would spoil me. No chance! She gave up her good job to look after her sister's child. Only thirty years old, the sister. Tragic. Some sort of cancer. And look what they are doing to the old lady now. Don't even visit here regularly. Two cars, paid for with her insurance money, but do they take her out on a sunny day? You must be joking! Too busy, much too busy, always. But she won't have anything said against them. Makes excuses for them instead.

They are young, I am old
she says.

I avoid talking to them now. Get too angry. Especially after they sold the house. Her house, as far as I am concerned. She was in hospital when they did it. I still can't believe it. A stroke is bad enough, but that must have broken her heart. Alright, it was the nephew's house, his mother's house, she told me, defending their appalling behaviour again, but surely, her sister had wanted her to live there until the end of her days. It was her home really, wasn't it.
They even sold her furniture, for a song, everything.

Too old-fashioned
they said.

Furniture she had brought back from the Far East. Furniture she treasured and polished every day, especially that wonderful hand-carved chest from China

Everything was sold very fast. No wonder! They needed a deposit for their posh, new house on the outskirts of town. Not a thought, how the old lady would feel. She could live with them, they said. A convenient baby-sitter, more like. She tried it. Didn't need to tell me she was unhappy there. Not that she would have complained. Much too loyal, as always. Wasn't at all well either. No blame, never any blame, only love. Then she started to fall a few times. Dizzy spells. Old people have them, don't they? She even fell down the stairs. Bruises all over. That's why they had to put her into the nursing home, they said. For her own safety, they said.

Don't really know why we got on so well. Always have. Not much in common really, and she is so much older. It started with my pea soup, I think. The smell must have drifted into her back kitchen over the backyard wall. It reminded her of her mother's home-made soups, she said. I gave her some every week after that. On Saturdays usually.

We never say all that much to each other. Don't need to. Respect each other's privacy. Have a good laugh, and a cup of Earl Grey together, now and again. Send Xmas cards, that sort of thing, but not in and out of each other's houses every five minutes, no, not that.

And now? Well, I visit her, when I can. After all, she looked after our house every year when we went on holiday. Watered the plants. Fed the cat. Those who care for her in the home are friendly enough. She wouldn't complain anyway. Keeps her dignity and pride. Love for her sister's son and now for his little daughter keeps her going in spite of everything. Mind you, she has a word or two to say about the 'nurse' sometimes. That's only natural, isn't it? She knows what she tells me in confidence doesn't go any further. Everyone needs someone to moan to, don't they?

Two official-looking men were with her last week when I arrived at the Nursing Home. Last Tuesday, it was.

The gentleman are from Littlewoods Pools
she said, introducing them to me.
I've won the jackpot.

She likes a good laugh and a joke. Of course, I didn't want to pry into her business so I laughed along with her explanation.

What would you do with all that money, if it was true?
I asked her later on, after the men had gone.

You know what I would do
she said.

Give it all to my sister's boy and his little family, especially to the baby, no use to me, is it?

The baby is two this month. She is hoping that they'll come to see her. Asked me to buy one of those expensive dolls they advertise on the telly. She died that afternoon. Her last words to me were:

Don't let me down, Mary, please.
I didn't understand at all what she meant at the time.

Since then there has been her will. She left the pools' jackpot to me. All of it. I know what she expect me to do with it. Can hear her words now:

I would give it all to my sister's boy and his little family, especially the baby.

Hope I am strong enough to honour her wish, even if, except for the little one, they don't deserve a penny of it.

And anyway, my lucky number is twenty-five. She told me so.

THE FINAL EXPERIENCE
John Tirebuck

Even on hearing again, the wet slap of a sea surge through wrack-strewn rocks, and the curfew of a curlew, I half knew that any attempt to recapture what I had lost, was begging the impossible.

Still, I caught the scents retrieved from mind on Firth of Lorn: clear, cold sea, foam of peaty brine, flotsam in decay, bivalve shell and iodine. Only the held-aloof noses of inquisitive seals and floating, wooden fish boxes were missing. It wasn't just melancholy that forced the sting of salty tears to my sea-grey, sea-blue eyes.

Overwrought and struggling with my emotions, I was in the one place that I had ever found contentment. I should have stayed then, but no: I was obliged to try to improve my lot. I could have been content with this paradise.

It broke her heart when I left. She cried, inconsolable. I tried to write, to phone, but her mother . . . I was cast out of their lives for the hurt I'd caused.

She married, of course, as did I, yet I wonder still, if she thinks fondly of her first pure love: unblemished and tender?

An evening chill had entered the air and a breeze accompanied the turning tide. Standing beneath the canopy of the Gem Box, I watched a couple hurry by, arm in arm, clutching a fish supper.

'People watching;' was one of our things. We would hide in Rena's car and study the antics of American tourists, as if we were anthropologists on a dark continent.

Aware of my other hunger, I would stand again in the warm, bright fish bar, with its moist, hissing, vinegar-scented air, and study faces: imagine how she must look today, twenty years on.

Turning away from the sea, I rose with the road to the centre of town, but instead of the fish bar where drunken Danny had explained to me how the Haggis were caught, there now stood a well-established Indian restaurant.

Moving along, without my supper, long-shore drift took me past the Great Western: the setting for a dozen twice-told tales. Where was Archer now?

'Only two things smell of fish, and one of them's fish,' he'd say.

What had become of old Danny with his bruised and battered whore, or Big Jim with his dreams of owning a garage in Australia? Did he ever pay off his drinking debts?

I returned to my hotel room, to whiskey and to haunted, nightmarish sleep.

Next morning, I met cold reality with a start. It permeated me with the gut-sick feeling that one experiences on emerging into the day of a vital examination, or in those minutes before pre-medication takes effect.

I looked around my hotel room, or should I say, my partitioned half of a once splendid Victorian morning room, now architecturally disfigured, an incongruous shower cubicle occupying one boxed corner.

Rising to the sounds of my neighbour's ablutions, I gazed out of my half of the window, and mused on the meanings of my dream whilst looking down on my beloved town. No augur would be needed. No oracle, or Joseph in his many colours, would be required for this one. Part of the answer to my troubled sleep lay before me.

Answers bled from the weeping clouds above my dearest memories. Visit 'The Oban Experience', the sign rashly proclaimed. Oh no. I had shared that experience and this was not it. No more than one could experience sleeping with a secret love, by placing her photograph under a pillow.

I laughed and cried with this community. I taught their children, enjoyed their music and their dance, and sadly, grieved for one or two.

I was there on a midnight, mid-summer sunset, when the fleet came in. That phalanx of fathers and brothers, uncles and sons, all laden with fish: silver fish to be packed in ice, crashing down in bursting bags, shovelled quickly into holds and all the townsfolk were there. Not the tourists who inhabit the lower streets in summer, but the real people whose homes looked down from their crowned hill above the bay. From

Ardconnel Road and Laurel Road; Gracies, Robertsons and McPhees: the people of my memories. Oh yes, I was there, and the memories linger like the scents of the sea in my dreams.

'The Oban Experience' could not have been less of what it proclaimed to be. Steel piles and concrete, instead of barnacle encrusted oak, alive with eels below the boards, and visited when the catch was in, by brave and opportunist seals.

Gone, the fish to Russia, Spain and Japan. Gone, the boats. Gone, the children that I had taught, to city jobs, not vocations. Rootless now, they are tumbleweeds. Gone too, the dreams of two preceding generations: one dying of despair, the other, resigned.

Lothlorian has faded and the concrete egg-carton, houses only pictures of a fleet.

Skipping breakfast's watered porridge, I found myself outdoors, scouring the faces in the street for a hint of recognition. Breathless,
I climbed the cliff steps of Jacob's ladder to the upper town. I met no one that I knew, or remembered me from days when she raced me to the top.

Passing through the portals of McCaig's Tower, I stood in our favourite window space and scanned the urban landscape below.

The little bay where winkles and feathered sea-slugs lived by blennies and blue-rayed limpets, was now the grey concrete platform for an artless storage depot decked out in railway depot drab.

My gaze moved to Lochavaulin playing fields, devoid of shinty-playing children, but scarred instead with small, failing businesses, housed in concrete bunkers, gardened about with the litter of industry and the mobile dwellings of New Age travellers, or old World Tinkers.

But what is this beyond? Out towards Lonan and Kilmore, ghastly grey tenements, thrown up for the city influx of paper-pushers and the dispossessed. Where has it gone, the scene of my youth: my youth?

Wait! Was that Catriona? I'll swear it was. Boyish figure, hair wild in the wind, jeans and a baggy Arran, running for the bus. She's not changed. Just as I remember her, coming out of school. Oh no . . . I am mistaken.

This place and its people have become suspended in my quirky time perception. All has moved on without me. I feel betrayed.

Late afternoon now and the angle of the light rims everything with black in true pop-up book style.

Here I am at 'Myrtle Bank', looking for Mary: laughing Mary of Tiree. But Gary and Teddy are buried with their bones and the house no longer smells of dogs.

My old land-lady is much older now. She knows me not. No sign of recognition in her benevolent, time-worn face. Geraniums in the powdered paint conservatory are clones, I'm sure, of those I used to know.

Perhaps my moving experience was just so much trivia in her timescape. I chose to believe that her mind has gone. At least then, she will not share my sense of loss.

Descending the snail-shell spiral of Rockfield Road, I pass my old school, without looking and quickly cross to the sea's margin. In fact, I do not stop until Dunollie Monument is reached. Studying the skyline, I am reassured that some things do not change.

I sit through peach and pink, purple and indigo, red and gold, ranged with graduated silhouettes and then perhaps I blink, because I miss the final flash of duck-egg green as the sun is quenched in the boiling sea.

'Got a cigarette pal, or some spare change?'
Feeling intimidated by the threatening presence, I hand over coins and quickly move away. Hairs on the back of my neck confirm that I am being followed. I sense danger, then shock, but there is no pain.

Now, at this unknown time, I seem to be hanging in the atmosphere. It is night. I see Argon, Neon, Xenon light, lying in puddles on the wet cobbles. Although I am not moving, I perceive a change in position. I am gliding off along the wharf, passing the seamen's mission, suspended in the gathering gloom, unbreathing yet aware.

I am drifting like a sea-fret or a dark balloon, floating, yet still thinking. Hovering, unblinking, I see wooden boxes and smell the staleness that lingers like the smell of fish on Archer's fingers.

I can almost pick them out: herring, mackerel, halibut, blood.

But what is this? A drunk perhaps, face down, contorted. He looks familiar. I feel that I should know him, but no.

The wharf is not so close now. The edges of my consciousness are less distinct. Something I knew is fading and yet the dawn approaches.

NATUREPARCS
John Doyle

'Look at them, looking at us! Yeuch, it's a bit creepy, I feel my skin crawling. Do you think they can understand what we're saying?'
'I doubt it, they're pretty docile and unintelligent really.'

At that, one of the creatures made a move to approach us, so I wound up the window and started the engine.

Our visit to the National Park had not gone entirely to plan and I was beginning to regret my earlier enthusiasm. The 'Natureparcs' company which ran the operation, tightly controlled access to the wildlife and it felt quite claustrophobic to be herded round the reserve.

As a zebra, I felt it was my duty to take the wife and children out in our 4x4 off-road Land Rover and see what the authorities were doing with the few humans left alive. After all, we paid our taxes and were entitled to see if they were being properly spent. The Prime Minister, Mr Giraffe, had explicitly promised that the environment would be at the heart of his administration: 'ecology, ecology, ecology' he had intoned in that famous party conference speech, while munching suavely on a mouthful of eucalyptus leaves.

My better half, the mare of my life, had however, expressed a healthy scepticism towards our leader's promises:
'Neigh chance, I wouldn't trust that spotted loon as far as I could throw him' had been her exact words, as I recall.

Anyway, we took him at his word and followed his advice to visit the new National Park in the Lake District. You wouldn't think that in this day and age, the third century after the flood, that there were still humans left alive. They survived on the mountain tops: Ararat, Olympus, Rushmore, Ben Nevis. These old names we learned when we discovered their books after the people disappeared, drowned beneath the waves.

The civilisation which grew up as we colonised a post-diluvian landscape, was, of course, shaped in our own image: kinder, gentler, softer. Some horses said it was more 'feminine' than the masculine culture of the bipeds whom we replaced.

Yes, of course I understand that old phrase 'Nature, red in tooth and claw', but this Darwin chap, with his Old Testament beard and harsh, competitive theories - he never appealed to us horses when we finally understood *The Origin of Species*. What about love, mutual respect, comradeship and compassion? How could the humans forget about this? Actually, when we arrived at the 'Natureparc', near the old lake of Windermere, I wanted to ask one of the exhibits why they hated each other so. But Chevaline, my partner, wisely counselled caution:

'What answer would satisfy you, my ribboned rogue? Leave these poor wretches to their fate. Give them space, they have endured, survived . . . Let that be enough.'

As she nuzzled my neck in the car, I blushed red on my white skin and saw the reason in her eyes. Besides what good would it do our foals to learn of the faults of others? Let us be horses and let men be men, we can be no other.

Indeed perhaps as zebras - a 'cross-breed', as our Arabian cousins half-mockingly call us - we can have a special insight into the plural, open, multi-faceted nature of life. No animal - or human, for that matter was ever pure, ever wholly white, black, brown, red, yellow, male, female, young or old. We carry our opposites, our enemies, inside our souls and if we are wise, we learn to cherish our differences.

'Typical lily-livered, woolly liberal hogwash (snort)!'

That's *she who must be obeyed* again, putting her oar in, just in case I get carried away with the rhetoric. Love the sound of my own voice I do, ever since I learned to speak, I practise in front of a mirror. Now that's one human invention of which I certainly approve . . . where was I? Ah yes, just because I don't wear a saddle, doesn't mean my wife doesn't have a good grip of my reins. Just as well really, silly old stallion!

One human of whom I heartily approve, read his books avidly, is a writer, cleric, wit and some would say, misanthrope. Ah, but he loved animals, horses especially - old Dean Swift. Jonathan, as I like to call him, was a wily Irish rascal who immortalised our gentle species in his masterpiece, *Gulliver's Travels*. We're too good for our own good, according to him - I can live with that. However, I'd rather not delve too deep into his essay, 'A Modest Proposal' - a satire on cannibalism and racial prejudice (whinny). We squeamish equines don't have stomachs for that sort of strong stuff, must be all the grass we eat, never got the hang of all that carnivorous human nonsense. Why, we have enough problems coping with the ravenous chimps who now proliferate. No problems with gorillas though - a lovely, sweet, gentle bunch, very unsimian, I'd say.

But what about our children - how did we protect our colts and foals through the dark years of the flood, you ask? Well, we took them onto higher ground, away from the remaining humans. Then, when the waters receded, we emerged from remote caves, barns on upland farms, long deserted. We crossed continents, sought out mountainous isles; we scavenged, we ate grass, fodder, learned to adapt, survive and prosper.

I'll tell you, when we first learned to read, two books which really helped us were George Orwell's novel *Animal Farm* - great writer, poor human being; and the collected works of Edwin Muir - especially his poem 'The Horses' - what a sad man.

The first book taught us which mistakes to avoid - never let the pigs take over. The second taught us how to live in harmony with the remaining humans after a cataclysm. Then, slowly but surely, we took responsibility for our own lives, took command of our own and of the earth's destiny.

So, now we have arrived back home from our day out. Home to our hill farm. OK young 'uns, out ye get. It's good to be home, back in the bosom of the family, you might say. But what a terrible warning - what disaster might await us too - the day we went to 'Natureparcs' to visit the animals in the zoo.

ANGEL'S KISS
Jane Darnell

The petals were wilting from the heat of her hand. She was not too sure of how many there were. She carefully placed a finger in her mouth leaving a deposit of spittle on the nail. Plucking a petal she stuck it over her nail and smiled at the result with pleasure; it was like a butterfly. Another followed until even her thumb was decorated. There were two petals left on the dismembered flower, pale pink ruffles with purple edges. The pollen made her nose twitch and she sneezed as she twisted the flower around on the remnant of the stalk. She threw it down and sat on her bicycle, it had been left out in the rain. She would not get smacked for having wet knickers from rain.

She fluttered her fingers so that the petals waved gently, then swooping her whole hand vigorously she made an imaginary bird. She sighed as two fell off, another bent and ripped and she scraped it off with her fingernail.

The babble of voices from within the house drifted out through the open back door. They became louder and higher in pitch. She could hear that woman who said she was her new mummy screaming down the telephone.
'You must come home immediately Brian.' She was crying as she was talking. 'No not later, now!' her voice sounded emotional and loud, she frowned that was no way to talk to her daddy.

Her aunt Polly who had arrived some ten minutes ago was crying and making no sensible conversation at all. Waste of time her coming around, aunt Polly had not even looked for her when she had arrived, but had rushed straight into the house and started crying. Adults were strange.

Daddy did not talk to her so much now, not since they had got that radish wrapped up in a shawl they called Hugh after a film star. That had annoyed her. Why should the new baby, their baby they called it, be given a film star's name, when she, when she had had both proper mummy and daddy had been called Amy after her grandmother?

They had expected her to hold the radish and help choose his clothes after his daily bath. He looked like Jemima her doll, except that he smelt like something that had been left too long in the fridge and he sicked up milk that smelt worse than when Smugs the cat from next door peed by the mint bed.

She cycled round in a circle following the little crazy paving path that led down to the garden shed. A movement made her look up and there was Smugs sitting on top of the shed. She waggled at finger at him. 'Smugs, cuddly Smugs come and see me.' He leapt to greet her. 'You are not cross with me are you Smugs?' She stroked him gently and he purred contentedly. 'Do you like riding on the bike Smugs? Shall we go for a little ride?' She plopped him into her lap and sang to him. 'Pussycat, pussycat where have you been?'

Out of the corner of her eye she saw the back door move and a foot appear. 'Ha.' Someone was going to come and see how she was for a change. She rode behind a laurel bush and waited to be found practising the Bee-Bo silently.

No one came along the path. The neighbour from over the road came out through the door and put something into the dustbin. What on earth was she doing in Daddy's kitchen? Another one who liked to come and pet the radish. No one cared where she was at all. They probably did not even know that she was in the garden. Perhaps she should run away. Would Grandmother look after her? Perhaps proper Mummy would come back and fetch her. It was very bad of her to go away. It was bad enough when she stayed in bed all day and would not play. Then one day when she, Amy, had come home from Grandma's, Mummy had gone. Daddy had cried and said she had gone to heaven. She had cried as well when Mummy did not come when she called her. Why had she gone away to heaven when her little girl needed her? It was a distant memory now and she did not cry anymore.

There was nothing to do in this garden. Daddy has packed the swing away when they had moved from their old house to live with new Mummy and had not put it up again. She had asked him but he always replied he was too busy, but would do it as soon as the weather got better. That was ages ago, it was all Radish's fault. Ever since he had arrived no one had time for anything.

A car turned into the driveway. She could see the roof, red and shiny peeping over the lapboard fence that separated the garden from the road. Daddy was home. Perhaps she would ride once more around the garden before she went indoors to see him. Maybe when she did she would watch television.

Perhaps it was not a good idea to go into the house, the noise was getting worse. She had supposed that now Daddy had arrived all would be well again, but he was shouting too, a sort of strangled wailing shout.

They put interesting programmes on the television. Like very early this morning before new Mummy was up. They had a doll like Radish, only a little bigger and they were teaching adults how to do mouth to mouth resus . . .something. Anyway whatever it was it looked very easy. All you had to do was pinch the nose and hold the head back so the throat came upwards in an arch then blow quickly into the mouth.

It was a shame they did not explain everything. If she could write like Daddy, she would and ask them what happened if you accidentally leant on their stomach and made them lose their early morning dinner. Then again not every baby would have had dinner like Radish had. He was always being sick anyway, so it probably made no difference. Still that was television for you. Only gave you half of the story as Daddy said every night when he read the newspaper.

Another car was drawing up; she was not sure to whom this one belonged. She stood up tall on the pedals pulling Smugs up onto her shoulder like a scarf. A tall thin man with a black bag like Daddy takes to work with his papers in, steps from the car. He is in a hurry, he has not bothered to shut the car door and runs into the house, his feet banging up the stairs. I am most definitely not going into the house with him there.

Daddy is calling me. I knew he would. 'Where are you my little angel?' he calls. That's me. He wants to tell me something very sad about Radish he says. I shall pretend that I cannot talk. Just like you Smugs, just like you. Except you Smugs will know that my silence is not through shock.

FLY BY NIGHT
Melanie M Burgess

'Come in officer. I'm so sorry I wasn't available this morning.

Not a morning person really. Getting too old for wandering about at night.

Routine enquiry you say, oh, about that poor girl. I saw that on the news, dreadful business.

Young people aren't safe to go out of an evening. Too bad.

Yes I was at that club as a matter of fact. I was hoping to do a bit of business. Colleague never turned up. So there I was amongst all these youngsters.

No, I didn't stay long. Not once I realised my contact wasn't coming. Must have found someone to supply it cheaper. Way of business I'm afraid.

Could you have his name? I must have his card somewhere, his name was Peterson I think.

Nice chap. Didn't think he was the type to let you down.

No I haven't been here long. Purely business. I live in the States, but the firm does quite a bit of business here.

Actually my parents were Romanian, I was educated in England, Oxford. Are you an Oxford man officer?

No, shame, wonderful atmosphere, I loved my Oxford days. One doesn't lose the values.

Just as well living in America. Do you know America well?

Holidays you say, with the family? Oh I see, you aren't married.

Sporting holidays? Am I right? Yes, it's a great place for sport. Cut-throat for business but I enjoy that.

No, my business is in New York but I live in a small town outside the city. I like small towns, you get to know people better.

Would you like some tea? Yes? I'll put the kettle on.

What were you saying officer? I can't hear in that kitchen when the kettle is on.

Not much furniture, You're right. I was told the place was fully furnished by the agents.

Too late once you've signed the lease, I arrived to find this. Still a bit of sparsity looks creative don't you think?

I'll get that tea. You'll have a biscuit as well?

Here we are, nothing like a cuppa to put things in perspective.

No, back to the furniture, it's enough to suit my purposes. I'm only here for a couple of weeks

And if I happen to meet a nice woman, there is a large bed. I'm sure we're men of the world here.

You're right, a businessman like myself doesn't really require the creature comforts.

Or doesn't get them more likely. Not when the firm is paying. They will wine and dine clients but let an employee ask them for something.

I expect it's the same with the force isn't it? Budgets and all that.

It does mean you have narrow limits to work in. Try telling that to the accountants.

It's not their child lying bleeding from the jugular.

I think I got that from one of the tabloids. You know how colourful they can be.

But back to the money situation. When I first started with this company the sky was the limit.

Yes cut backs. It's the same the world over. The big bosses can still take their cut though hey?

Look at the job you do and probably paid half my salary.

I don't think that is right. I don't have to lay my life on the line.

What business am I in? Oh didn't I say? Computers, isn't everyone?

Solving more crimes using them? Is that right? What do they call them, forensic profiles? I thought it was only the FBI went in for that.

No, I haven't personally had contact with the FBI. I think one of our branches supplied one of their branches with computers.

I'm always sent to England because of my background. I suppose it's mostly London though. Shame that.

Have you ever been to Yorkshire? You should go there, Whitby in particular. A charming resort.

Yes I suppose I am wandering off the subject of the girl.

Someone thought they saw me talking to her you say.

Perhaps they did. I spoke to a few pretty girls that night.

I always chat up pretty girls, far too young for me of course. I don't need irate parents on my doorstep.

Oh I see she had no parents or close relatives. How sad. I can empathise with her. I'm in the same boat. All my family have passed on years ago.

And you? Oh dear. We are an unfortunate few or perhaps fortunate. Sometimes relatives can be a trouble.

What flight did I come over on? Now you are asking. I can't remember my name from one moment to the next.

It arrived in the morning. I flew from New York. A long journey that.

Only about six hours you think. It probably seems longer.

What movie did they show? The latest blockbuster just gone I assume. I never watch movies. They show people in a bad light.

I suppose the office might know, or I may still have the ticket folder somewhere. Can I come back to you on it?

I'm not the best person to ask for things like that, because I move about a lot. I don't keep things.

Yes, I suppose as a police officer you do hoard things. Not me. I like to be as sparse as possible when I fly.

You're jumpy this evening officer. Bit late for house calls maybe, you saw something pass the window.

Oh, it would have been a bat. I think they are nesting or something. I've seen several since I've been here.

You thought it was trying to get in the window. I doubt it. They have a keen sense of radar.

Maybe they are in the eaves of this building.

I know quite a bit? Well I have an interest in bats. I find them rather fascinating creatures.

You aren't very satisfied with my answers, I'm sorry about that. I hope this doesn't mean my staying here longer.

I was hoping to leave the day after tomorrow. The thermals are supposed to be just right.

Yes, I do say some strange things don't I. I come from a strange family I suppose.

You couldn't find me home during the day either. Not surprising I'm more of a night person.

You would be surprised at how many business deals are made at night-clubs or dinner parties. Get them relaxed and then go in for the kill. Metaphorically speaking of course.

They saw the girl leaving with me?

Who did? Oh witnesses. I don't know how anyone could see anything in that club, it was so dingy.

You feel tired. The tea probably. Tea is relaxing.

What did I put in the tea? A mild relaxant.

I could take you without it, we are extremely strong. I'm not in the mood for a fight tonight.

If you had waited one more day I would have been gone, flown back to the big city.

They have my description. Probably so, we're shape shifters as well of course.

They will have police at the airports. Now you are getting desperate. We can't produce our ticket voucher because we didn't have one. We can fly without a plane dear boy.

Don't worry about the girl. Her body has probably left the morgue by now. Of its own free will.

Do you want to see my fangs?'

DAIONE SHIE
Jack Sharp

Detective Constable Carthy, of the Garda, shook Nuala's hand as they met outside the chapel of rest.

'Another one,' she lamented with a touch of cynicism.

'Yes. But we'll get 'em yet. Did ye hear about the Sheehans' baby? Disappeared without trace,' he asked quietly as if not wishing others to hear.

'I did! She's at it again.' Nuala answered with a note of authority.

Constable Carthy suppressed a smile as they entered the chapel to pay their respects.

Dermot was the second young man to meet a mysterious death and the disappearance of the Sheehans' baby had intensified gossip around the town with the speed of a forest fire.

The good folk of Newbliss, nestling in the valley of the river, marking the border between the north and south of Ireland were infuriated by recent events. All were there to pay their last respects to young Dermot; standing solemnly around the coffin, shaking hands with the family and offering their condolences.

'We'll be investigating this thoroughly. Might be terrorists!' Constable Carthy whispered to Father John as he approached him with a handshake.

'We've not been affected by the troubles yet. I hope this isn't the start.' Father John replied solemnly.

Kate, overhearing them, said firmly, 'It's more likely the Daione Shie. Bridget, their queen, is deadly to her lovers. I often saw young Dermot away over the fields.' She spoke too loudly. Dermot's mother, hearing her comment, shouted angrily through her tears,

'How dare you insult my son and him lying here at peace before us.' All eyes turned towards Nuala as she replied sympathetically,

'Well! I'm sure Bridget'd make sure he died happy. I'm certain of that.'

Constable Carthy, sizing up the situation, grabbed Nuala's arm and amidst muted mutterings of dissent from those gathered near her, steered her gently to the exit.

'I tell ye, that lad was not killed by terrorists or murdered by others and not a mark on him,' she stormed at him as soon as they were outside.

'Now Nuala, will ye quieten ye gab a bit?' he asked anxiously looking around furtively.

'Indeed I'll not! We all know what the Daione Shie are capable of. It's only the youngsters that don't believe,' she answered angrily.

'Come now, I'll walk ye home.' Constable Carthy took Nuala's arm as he spoke. They walked up the main street together, discussing the matter. He assured her that the death of young Dermot and the disappearance of the Sheehans' baby would be fully investigated.

Next morning Nuala went shopping in the town bursting with the need to talk to all she met about recent happenings. She was convinced, as were most of her generation, that the Daione Shie were responsible. Their parents and grandparents before them had all told stories about the adult fairies of Castle Carrigh. But the younger generation were sceptical, feeling that terrorist or other criminal activity was more likely.

Nearing lunchtime, Nuala, fancying a glass of stout, went into McGinty's Bar. Farmer Kelly sat at the side of the fireplace, speaking as loud as usual. 'It's all of ten metres across; as perfect a circle as y'ever did see,' he said to his cronies gathered around him, arms awide to give emphasis.

'What colour?' asked someone with a hint of disbelief.

'Dark green with wee toadstools round the edge,' he answered positively.

'Must have been there some time,' another said thoughtfully

'No! It wasn't there yesterday. Appeared this morning; plain in the rising sun,' Farmer Kelly went on with assurance.

Nuala listened intently to it all before she interrupted, addressing them from the bar, 'That'll be where Queen Bridget and the adult fairies of peace danced their lament at midnight.' All turned to look in her direction.

'Rubbish!' a youngster exclaimed loudly.

'Well let's go and find out,' she said resolutely.

Farmer Kelly agreed so they all made their way to the field and there it was; a fairy ring. He swung his arm around as he pointed to the edge of it; turned to Nuala and asked, 'Now wouldn't ye think that if fairies had danced here the toadstools would have been flattened?'

'Indeed I would not! Queen Bridget and her fairies are of our stature, but they move with the lightness of angels. That's where they are different and this is their sign,' Nuala answered, drawing all the authority she could from the very depths of her beliefs.

Many nodded their heads in silent approval but the more vocal expressed their disbelief with such comments as; nonsense: cattle: the weather and other realities.

'Listen!' she yelled back at them, 'They dwell in the rath up by the Castle Carrigh. Let's go up there. See what other proof they've left us.'

Farmer Kelly said he'd work to do, others said it was pointless, but the majority felt that there was a need for more drinking and talking before this mystery was solved. Off they all went, back to McGinty's; leaving Naula to walk home alone with her beliefs.

None of this directly explained Dermot's death or the disappearance of the Sheehan's baby. Constable Carthy didn't get far with his investigations either.

Meantime, Nuala's niece, Roisin, was due to have her first baby and the big day arrived. Nuala rushed round to assist with the delivery of a beautiful little girl. They were just making mother and baby comfortable when Sean, Roisin's husband, returned home. His face, a mixture of apprehension and wonder, said it all. 'Did you see that beautiful lady down by the poplar tree?' he asked excitedly.

Nuala was quick to respond, 'We've all been too busy with your baby daughter. But that'll be Queen Bridget of the fairies. She usually visits at these times to welcome the newcomer.'

'I'm sure I saw someone,' Sean said doubtfully.

'Did she say anything?' Nuala asked seriously.

'No.' She just cradled her arms, as if holding a baby and then pointed to the town,' Sean answered, acting out her actions.

'Yes, that was her. She was telling you that your baby had arrived and will work in town. Probably a nurse at the hospital,' she said thoughtfully.

Father John, hearing Nuala's comment, took her aside. 'You mustn't indulge in such speculations about spirits, other than those of the Saints,' he admonished quietly but firmly.

Well! thought Nuala, after all I've done for the Church: Blessings: Masses at home and regular confessions. She was very upset, not seeing any difference between her fairies and the Saints. Nevertheless, that evening she went to confession, gave thanks for the safe arrival of the baby, discussed her feelings about Bridget and the fairies, did her penance and resolved to visit the wrath and Castle Carrigh as soon as she had time.
If she hadn't then the circumstances were such that she'd have to find it.

Constable Carthy was surprised to meet Nuala entering the Police Station as he was leaving for his night patrol. 'Hello, what are you doing out so late?' he asked with concern.
'I've decided to check up on Queen Bridget and her fairies of peace. They're usually about in the twilight,' she answered abruptly.
'I didn't think they were about much before midnight,' he queried.
'Do you know, I think you're right. That's when they're much more likely to be about. They're different from us in that respect as well,' she answered, once more asserting her beliefs.
Constable Carthy's face took on a serious pose. He didn't relish the idea of Nuala going up to the wrath alone at midnight, but before he could respond she went on, 'Will ye come with me?'
'I'd better. Meet me at the top of the town at 11 o'clock,' he answered, wondering whether he'd done the right thing.

It was a tidy walk from the top of the town to the wrath and Castle Carrigh but they made it just before midnight. The moon was very bright, lightening the darkness as they approached, so they moved into a nearby wood and waited.
'Hear that?' whispered Nuala, responding to a noise from the Castle.
'Yes,' Constable Carthy replied, raising his finger to his lips.

The noises they heard were muffled, a muted musical shuffling or was it digging? There were signs of activity and shaded lights in the vicinity of the Castle ruins.

They crouched in the undergrowth wondering whether this was it; either the Diaone Shie dancing another lament or terrorists burying their weapons. What would they do next?

'We need back-up.' Constable Carthy flicked the switch of his mobile 'phone as he spoke; quickly sending the message.

Constable Carthy deployed his reinforcements, such as they were, around the Castle so that they could move in from all directions. Upon his signal they rushed in, flashlights piercing the darkness, covering the last few yards in seconds. The muffled sounds took on a more realistic tone of line dancing music.

It stopped suddenly and there they were: youngsters from all over the County, gathered together in couples dancing and canoodling or groups drinking. The band of violin, fiddle and accordion players were grabbed as they made way to the wood. Others shot off into the shadows but most just stood and stared in disbelief.

'What's this then?' Constable Carthy shouted, irritated that he'd called for help to tackle a Ceilidh.

'Looks like the Colleens and Gossons is having a party!' a hefty colleague replied before any of the youngsters could.

The party over, a few names were taken as a matter of routine and the crowd gradually dispersed into the night.

Nuala and Constable Carthy walked slowly back to town.

'You and your Queen Bridget,' he said sarcastically.

'Well, that's her way. She encourages the youngsters to dance together in peace, joy and love. You need have no worry about terrorists while she's about.'

'But what about poor Dermot and Sheehan's baby?' he asked with a touch of professionalism.

Naula thought awhile, hesitated, then answered confidently,

'Young Dermot died happily in Bridget's arms after making love. She's known to respond in that way. A great way to go to be sure. I think you'll probably find that Sheehan's baby is with its grandparents in Donegal. The Sheehan's have enough on their plate with the other six children. They'll have sent their wee one off; saying nothing to anyone because they don't want people to know their business.'

Constable Carthy had a look of approval on his face as he put his arm on Nuala's shoulder and said quietly, 'I think I might have another word with them.'

Those responsible for Dermot's death were never arrested.
Farmer Kelly has quite a few more fairy rings in his fields.
Nuala's niece, Roisin, had an extra visitor at the birth of her second child: down by the poplar tree.

Newbliss is at peace now but still has its share of strange happenings and Detective Constable Carthy always makes a point of discussing them with Nuala.

IMPOSSIBLE WISH
Danny Coleman

The crematorium was silent, the day warm and sunny. The gathered people quiet and thoughtful. Then . . . the lid lifted off my father's coffin and out he jumped! Some people fainted. What on earth was happening? He looked immaculate in a crimson suit with red and white spotted bow tie! Certainly not his usual attire but then I guess you could say this day was something special to him and unforgettable to us! Why would he have done this? What perverse logic made him think this a good idea? Did he not realise we all thought him dead? Didn't he know how sad we all felt without him? He walked up to me first, 'Millicent, you know I've told you many times how I'd like to make your wishes come true. Well! I just have!' I was only ten years old and didn't understand at all, he just hugged and kissed me saying, 'You will.' Then he moved to my brother Timothy, 'How's it going son?' he said. My brother, like many people in the congregation, burst into tears, he just couldn't believe it. Our father, who definitely art not in heaven, was smiling broadly at everyone he made eye contact with saying, 'Alright you old buggers.' Then he walked to the front of the church, saying loudly as he went, 'Never liked these places much anyway.' He duly gave us this explanation.

'Since my own mother died I've wished so many times she was still alive but I knew it couldn't be. If only that wish could have come true I would have cried a bathful of happy tears and laughed till I needed tranquillisers to stop the pains in my stomach from ending my own life prematurely. I have felt the same about many other people in my life who have died. I guessed other people felt the same way sometimes so I faked my own death simply to make the impossible wishes of some people here come true. A wish you would not have thought ever possible even in your wildest dreams. This was one of my dreams, to return to life just for the people here who were going to wish I was still here. As you know I won eight million pounds on the lottery last year. Even though I'm not dead my will still stands, I need neither the house nor its contents or my car. I am going to travel the world till I die a more permanent death. On the way out you can collect five thousand pounds each and a copy of my travelling agenda for the next year. I hope to see some of you soon. I am sorry for the sad feelings I know you must have experienced but I'm back so be happy and meet me somewhere or other on the planet I love so much.'

Some people never forgave my dad, I forgave him a split second after he spoke. I knew how much he'd loved his mother and why he'd done this. He'd pre-empted some people's wishes, including mine and made them come true before they had even thought about wishing for them. What foresight and imagination. What a way not to go. I'll still wish my dad was alive after he really dies but having it come true once was unbelievable, unforgettable, weird and wonderful. Thanks Dad, nice one.

LITTLE ACTS OF KINDNESS
David Rowan Walker

The tall man in the trench coat stood on the street corner, watching the traffic. The road was busy, but then at one o'clock in the afternoon it always was. The man was middle aged, with receding hair, a longish face, with just a very average look about him. He was the sort of person in fact, whom one would look at and just moments later forget what he looked like.

The man's attention moved to the numerous pedestrians who were mostly hurrying along the side walk, although some were stopping briefly to glance in nearby shop windows. His eyes flickered narrowly as he watched the mass of people racing past him; some tall, some short, some fat and others thin. A sea of colours and faces.

It had started to drizzle. His face formed a smile; he had been right to wear his raincoat, he thought. He never took any chances, and why should he; if the forecast was for rain, then there was a good possibility there would be rain! He was always so careful, so very, very careful.

The man's eyes scanned the crowd. It was then that he noticed the crippled man coming towards him slowly on crutches. The elderly cripple was shabbily dressed, with one of his trouser legs pinned up behind his knee. The crippled man approached slowly and his laboured breath could be heard loudly as he drew level with the tall man.

The tall man studied the cripple thoughtfully' he guessed that he must be past retirement age, and he surmised by the old man's appearance that his quality of life was most likely extremely poor indeed. He imagined that the man would be living on benefits in a small, cheap bed-sitter with just a television for company. He wondered how he had lost part of his leg. Maybe it had been lost during the war, or maybe as a result of an accident? He couldn't begin to guess, he only knew by the cripple's appearance and by his laboured breath as he struggled with his crutches that he was living a pathetic existence and that his quality of life would probably never improve.

The cripple continued on his way, without even a glance at the tall man. The tall man watched him pass and then followed a few paces behind him. A few hundred feet further along the pavement the cripple stood and turned to face the road; he was going to cross over, but had to wait because of the continual stream of traffic.

The tall man stood directly behind the cripple and watched the oncoming vehicles thundering along the road. His eyes scanned left and right along the pavement, and he glanced askance at all of the able-bodied people hurrying about their business. The crippled man seemed oblivious to all of the activity going on around him,' he just stood poised waiting for a break in the traffic.

The tall man waited patiently a little while longer. A bus was fast approaching the spot where he and the cripple were stood, and suddenly the moment he had waited for arrived. As the bus drew level with them, the tall man thrust his left hand forward into the cripple's back, giving him a violent push forward. It was done so quickly, so expertly, that no-one would have believed it possible. The cripple completely lost balance and fell into the road, straight into the path of the fast moving bus. The driver had had a few seconds to brake hard as he saw the cripple fall from the pavement, but the bus could not be stopped before it went completely over the man's body.

Chaos and desperate shouts for 'call for an ambulance', 'get the poor man help' followed, but the tall man knew it would be a complete waste of time. He knew that the cripple's death would have been instantaneous; he was good at judging death, as he had had a lot of practice in the past.

The tall man turned and moved away from the large crowd which had gathered and he thought to himself what a nice day it was turning out to be. After all, it was his little acts of kindness, like the one he had just done, that made the day worthwhile. He had put the cripple's miserable life to an end and that had to be a good thing.

He would try to do another act of kindness tomorrow; he usually did most days if he could - though of course it was not always possible due to other commitments he had.

His face broke into a happy smile, as his right hand gripped his walking stick handle tighter and he began to limp along the wet pavement, back the way he had come.

FLIGHT
Adie Leslie

I sat down in the seat next to the old woman, she was so old that her skin hung in wrinkles with the velvety smoothness of a new-born baby, and her frail shape folded neatly into the crook of the airplane seat. I had been allotted the empty seat beside her and took it reluctantly. Such an old body could cause problems on the journey. Idly I wondered why such an ancient should be making this long and tedious journey. I settled down and buckled my seat belt. Feeling her eyes upon me, I turned to meet the gaze of her bright, small eyes. The only young feature in that ruined face.

'I've been all over, you know' she said as if she had divined my previous reflections. I made a non-committal sound.

'Israel three times, South Africa once and then I went to Canada.' I was called upon to show some interest.

'How wonderful!' I gushed 'and especially at your age . . .' My voice wavered, was I insulting or patronising her? Surely she was at an age of which she could boast? I floundered. 'I meant, your health must be good, my grandmother couldn't . . .'

'When I told my doctor I was coming on this trip' she broke in before I could finish, 'I said there's nothing you can say to stop me. I'm going on it, even if it kills me! I told him, this is the one trip I've dreamed about since I was a little girl! No, if it kills me, I'm still going!' She chuckled.

'Do you know what he said to me?' He said 'it may well do that!' But I told him, 'so what does it matter?' There's a lot of dead people nowadays, all dead one way or another.'

She was silent for a time while I gathered my thoughts and then she tapped me on the arm, to draw attention.

'They weren't' going to let me fly when I got to the airport this morning' she confided 'a doctor took my blood pressure and said it was too high.' But I said 'it will kill me quicker if I don't go on my dream trip. I will be dead from disappointment.' I took full responsibility.

My neighbour, Noreen, brought me to the airport in her car and she wanted to take me home again. But I was firm, 'Don't fuss' I said. I've taken full responsibility.' She's a good person, a good neighbour, but she doesn't understand how I feel about this journey. How could she? Our experience of life is so very different.'

I knew that she wanted me to ask why she was going on his journey. 'Shall I fall into the trap? I asked myself. 'I suppose it could be interesting . . .' While I was debating the matter in this way, she said 'What a hustle and bustle this morning! I was all ready and packed days ago, but Noreen made me turn everything out to make sure I had everything I would need. Even my hand luggage, my holdall. I had to give way, an argument would have drained me of the energy I need for this trip. She does it for the best of possible motives, but sometimes I wish she'd leave me alone and if I suffered from neglect, at least it would be peaceful!'

I turned to smile at her, and saw her bright eyes glinting with humour. 'Why are you making this trip?' I asked dutifully and flushed with pleasure, she told me that her name was Golde Josephs and she was journeying to visit the small village in which her father had been born, near Riga in Latvia. 'Always my father talked about it. Such tales he told me! All my growing years I had a picture in my head of the green flower strewn fields, the lanes shaded by trees, the small house where he spent his boyhood. I know of all the people - the boys he played with, the girl who was his first love although he was too young, shy and clumsy to tell her of his feelings. The parents of his friends in the village, the grandparents . . . The ones who left and the ones who stayed.' She smiled at me, her skin wrinkling into a grimace. 'Those who stayed to perish will know from my return they are not forgotten. Yes, I want to see for myself the place where my father walked and breathe the air he breathed. It will be a kind of coming home for me.'

'What's the name of the village?' I asked, more for something to say than for any other reason.

'My father wrote it down for me before he died. The name is not easy to pronounce for an English tongue and I never learned my father's language' she finished sadly. 'He told me how to say it and when I was younger I think I knew, but now the name is only letters on a piece of paper.' She pulled a face. 'As soon as I put the paper down, pouf! The name goes out of my head.' She sighed. 'When I was younger I had a good memory.'

I did not know what to say, but was saved from making a reply by her asking me 'Can you find my holdall? It's under the seat.' I bent forward and lifted it towards her, balancing it on the arm of the seat while she rooted around in its interior, at last pulling out a bottle of brandy.

'I'll need it when I get to Russia' she said knowingly. 'Strong drink, that's the secret of a long life. I've had a glass of this every night before going to bed since Jack, my husband died, and I know that's what kept me so sprightly. I'm very lively, you know, people even younger than me can't keep up. How many people do you know who would go to Russia in the middle of winter? Noreen can't understand it. She thinks I'm mad!'

She offered me a drink but I refused for I had read that the drinking of alcohol in flight dehydrated the body. However, concerned that she might be offended at my refusal, I asked her to tell me more about her long life and she was only too pleased to oblige. She told me of her husband who had died painfully of cancer, her father, who had settled the family in Manchester and her own life in England. But she always returned to speak of her father's village, the place where he had been born and spent his childhood. A place to which she felt connected.

By now we were approaching Moscow airport.
'Pass my holdall to me again, please' she asked and once more I lifted it so that she could dig into a side pocket to bring out a shabby red diary. She handed it to me and said 'The bit of paper with the name of my father's village is in there. Find it for me, my dear, I can't see very well nowadays, a cataract in my right eye.'

I searched through the book. 'It's folded in there,' she urged. I turned the book upside down and shook it, but nothing fluttered out. I flicked through the pages again.

'It's not here!' I was embarrassed.

Golde reached out a trembling hand and seized the diary, she searched through it frantically, her hands shaking, her head twitching. At last she gave up, the notebook falling to her lap and leaned back in the seat, her face white, her eyes closed.

'Perhaps it has fallen into the holdall!' I said desperately so that she opened her eyes and jerked forward in her seat so that hopefully we could turn out the pocket of the holdall in which the red diary had been stored. Nothing. Now she cried out, rocking backwards and forwards within the seat belt.

'It was there! It was there! I put it there myself last night, before I went to bed!'

I searched in my mind for something to say.

'She made me, she made me turn everything out this morning. That's when it must have fallen from the book! I was in such a state and Noreen put everything back in the holdall!' She moaned, tears coursing down her wrinkled face. 'Neighbours are a curse!' she cried.

I looked around for help and caught the eye of the stewardess who crossed over to sort out the problem and thankfully I withdrew from the old lady's predicament.

The last glimpse I had of my travelling companion was at the airport. She was swaddled in blankets, sitting in a wheelchair, while a rep from the holiday company puzzled how to get the wheelchair down twenty steps and through passport control. Out of the windows of the airport lounge I could see the pine forest surrounding us and the deep cold snow like cumulus clouds. With a shiver I turned away, and hurried to collect my luggage.

WHODUNNIT
F Jensen

The residents were in full agreement, nothing like it had happened before in Lower Oxley, their sleepy, unspoilt village. Who would have thought it? they asked themselves - a streaker on their hallowed bowling green!

The bowling green, with its imposing pavilion, prize-winning flowerbeds and hanging baskets, was one of the focal points of the village, along with the church and public house. The locals were fiercely proud of it and although some of the younger ones found it mildly amusing most were incensed at what the Mothers Union President, Grace Palmer, referred to as 'an act of desecration.'

This unseemly incident occurred on Saturday when the A team were playing Hamsworth for the prestigious Beacher Cup. Hamsworth had won the cup for the last three years and had sent a strong team this year in an attempt to make it four in a row. Lower Oxley players, for their part, were determined to see that this time the cup was returned to its rightful owners. It was to be a keen contest.

The day was fine and clear with a cool, end-of-season feel about it. The match was well under way, with players on the green and spectators, male and female, grouped in front of the pavilion, when it happened. To everyone's amazement a lone, pale figure emerged from behind one of the rhododendron bushes on the right-hand side and ran briskly across the green. The figure was stark naked and plainly male. He then vanished behind the long pivet hedge on the left of the green, leaving the group of players rooted to the spot, transfixed, like figures in a tableau.

The next moment the spell was broken and there was an outburst of shouting, arm waving and finger pointing. It was almost ten minutes before the game was resumed. The visiting team took a somewhat detached view of the affair but the home team, winning up to that point, completely lost their composure, the match, and consequently the cup. Not surprisingly, the streaker was blamed for the defeat and members clamoured for him to be identified and apprehended. But he had disappeared completely.

Later, in the pavilion over tea and biscuits, the enquiries began - who was he? Where did he come from? Where did he go to? Why did he do it? Wilf Turner, captain of the men's team, took over the role of chairman. 'First things first,' he said. 'Did anyone recognise him or notice anything unusual about him?' Dorothy Maitland, captain of the ladies team, said she noticed he had very thin legs, adding lamely, 'If that's any help.' Betty Friar, who wore thick spectacles, thought it could have been a female streaker, like the ones seen on television being pursued by policemen. But Harvey Green, treasurer, suggested that, whoever he was, he must surely declare himself soon as presumably he did it to gain publicity.

As the discussion dribbled to an end the chairman expressed his dismay and disgust at such behaviour and promised to report the matter to the local police. The following evening an account of the incident appeared in the local newspaper.

From then on it became national news. It featured in newspapers and on television screens across the country, gaining strength as it received more publicity. Rumour and speculation about the phantom streaker abounded. It was joked that he might have been the trendy new curate they were expecting, putting in a premature appearance. There was a hint that he might be the owner of a shop recently opened and selling, amongst other things, a range of body lotions. One persistent rumour had it that he was a relative of one of the visiting team members, primed to put the home team off its stride. 'If so,' remarked one of the players, 'he certainly succeeded.'

The village was soon swarming with reporters, curious, as one explained, as to why someone who had courted publicity so blatantly should be so reluctant to reveal his identity now that he held centre stage.

Then there was a breakthrough of a sort. A single sock had been found at the very spot where the streaker had made his first appearance. It was a pale blue woollen sock of average size. This was displayed in the window of the Post office along with a note asking anyone who might recognise it to come forward - in complete confidence of course.

In time the affair quietly petered out. It was a three-day wonder, jostled into the background by events of greater importance. And so the mystery remained. But PC Lawrie, the village policeman, promised himself that he would see the case through to its conclusion, no matter how long it might take.

Some two years later Lawrie was browsing in the mobile library on one of its weekly visits. On one shelf he found a slim paperback, the title of which attracted his attention. It was The Modern Phenomenon of Streaking, by S W Laing. Lawrie opened it and noticed there were no date stamps on it. Apparently no one had yet taken the book out. No wonder, he thought, with a title like that. He began to read the Foreword:-

'In researching the subject I consulted public libraries, the Internet, and of course seasoned streakers themselves. I quickly became aware that I, personally, had no knowledge of what it actually felt like to 'streak' and realised that in order to do justice to the subject I had to experience it myself.

But while bona fide streakers generally sought publicity and expected to be caught, I on the other hand desperately wished to avoid both publicity and apprehension. While their naked sprints were carried out for fun, mine would be purely for scholarship. While theirs were usually impulsive acts, mine would require fine planning.

And so I planned to drive to a selected spot with an accomplice. There, to undress completely, leaving my accomplice to gather up my clothes. Then, oh shock, horror, to step out naked and walk, on shaking legs no doubt, through a group of open-mouthed players and spectators. And finally to continue on to an agreed hiding place to await, cowering, the arrival of accomplice and clothes.

I decided to perform (in the name of research, you understand) in some far-away village where I would be completely unknown. I thought it best to carry out this performance on a bowling green rather than on a more conventional cricket or rugby pitch in order to reduce exposure time.

That is how, one Saturday, I came to shock the good people of Lower Oxley and interrupt their friendly game of bowls. I hereby offer my sincere apologies to them and express my gratitude to them for their forbearance. Incidentally, inexplicably, I managed to leave one of my socks behind. If they are reading this, please can I have my sock back?'

P C Lawrie smiled to himself. So there it was, a public confession. He had his man at last and knew what needed to be done next. He rang Wilf Turner and suggested he should call an extraordinary meeting of the bowling club. He, himself, would attend to explain how he was now able to name the perpetrator. The meeting took place a week later. After Lawrie had made his opening remarks there was a general discussion centred around how the club should respond now that they knew the identity of the man who, many still thought, had brought undesirable publicity to the village and who probably played a part in their failure to regain the Beacher Cup.

It was an animated meeting and much ground was covered, but in the end there was unanimous agreement as to what action should be taken. A few days later the bowling club sent Mr Laing a new pair of pale blue socks, via his publisher, along with a notice of the club's forthcoming social evening. There was a warm invitation for him and partner to attend, which concluded with the words, 'Dress essential'!

THE LABURNUM TREE
Jenny Harrow

There's an hour before boarding the airport coach so I'm nipping down to the market in Beijing's North Dongsanhuah Road, Chaoyang District to buy a dagger.

Everyone in this massive city of 13 million is on the move - whether a peasant on a donkey taking leeks to market, or business tycoons chauffeur-driven in stretch limos with darkened windows.

The smog level is up to 436 I notice on a giant flickering electronic board - anything higher than 50 is above average, so it's no wonder the armies of women street sweepers look like gangsters with grimy scarves tied tight over mouths and noses.

I skirt a Kentucky Fried Chicken and the gleaming silver Swiss Bank, in front of which three old men in Chairman Mao caps squat on the pavement playing mah-jong, impervious to the relentless tide of feet flowing around them - mainly workers hurrying to and from the factories. Trishaws carrying cargoes of ancient women, bundles of broomsticks, a shitsou dog, self-conscious tourists, creak pass me in every direction, alongside hundreds of bicycles, often with two or even three people aboard. Sadly, amongst so many, there are a few kids - if you have more than one offspring here, you lose your work permit, ticket for survival. That's Government population control policy. Very efficient.

As usual since arriving here just five days ago, every one of my senses is kicked by sights, smells, sounds, tastes. My mind is numb with an overkill of sensations on this first incredible visit to mainland China.

I check my watch: 40 minutes to make the quick dash to an antiques shop just off to the left of Dongsanhuah Road. We'd already visited it earlier and in its rickety, dusty depths gorged ourselves on porcelain vases, terracotta figurines, copper bangles, silks and jade - all ridiculously cheap. I'd also spotted this bright little dagger, lethally sharp, in a wooden dragon-painted scabbard complete with red tassel. But reluctantly I'd chosen not to buy it for fear of getting caught up with it through Customs. On second thoughts, here I was deciding to risk it.

Mentally working out how I would knock the price down from 60 Yuan (less than a fiver) I am shamefully aware it would be worth at least treble that back home.

Lee, the tiny shopkeeper, immediately recognises me as I sweep over the raffia curtain and push aside his Evil Eye totems. He leaps off a wooden box, leaves of China Daily floating to the earth floor. 'You want more bracelets, china?' he asked eagerly, kow-towing.

I point to dagger, still there in the grimy glass frame.

Delighted, he pulls it out, wiping dust on his thin shirt. 'Original Cheng Dynasty. Velly, velly old. Only 65 Yuan.' The price has risen since yesterday - it's reassuring to know the party faithful are filthy capitalists too.

'I'll give you 40.' He groans and holds his head, peering through his fingers.

'50?'
'40.'
'45?'
'40.'

He sighs, kow-tows again and I know I've won. I finger the black handled dagger with its betasselled dragon scabbard and feel pleased if guilty. After a round of handshakes and blessings, I hurry to get back to the Landmark Hotel. Can't miss it I think - all 3000 rooms high (oh, and the crimson lift mats changed daily with 'Good morning it's Monday/Tuesday/Wednesday helpfully emblazoned in gold on each, just so you don't become totally disorientated.)

I head up the dirt road amid more shopsellers calling out and clutching at my clothes, but I am an old hand by now. 'No dollars - only sterling' I shout cheerfully back and they fall silent.

The shops are thinning out and there are only dingy housefronts and the odd alleyway up which I glimpse piles of old tyres, petrol cans, dustbins, the occasional rat. Ten minutes to go - I press on, beginning to regret my 'short cut'. It's quiet and empty here and the sun is fast fading behind yellow smog.

And this is when suddenly in front of me, appearing out of a left-hand doorway, comes a boy, probably late teens, scruffy, with the usual inscrutable black eyes. I stiffen sensing trouble. He leers up and lunges straight at the straw bag slung casually over my right shoulder.

Anger and terror rise in my throat. 'Piss off!' I screech. They usually do. This one didn't. Instead, he encircles me and pushes me up against a gnarled tree whose yellow laburnum blossoms dance crazily around us. He tries to grab the gold chain from my throat and with the other hand pinions me against the tree, eyes filled only with blackness, hot spicy breath choking me.

It's at this point I remember the dagger. I manage to shove my hand downwards and feel its cool handle and the dragon pattern scabbard. Courage comes and I close my fingers round it. Then, with a violent thrust, I yank the knife out of the scabbard. There's an infinitesimal moment when time stands still as I jerk the weapon up and out of my pocket.

The dagger glints briefly in the darkening air and then disappears as I thrust viciously between the boy's ribs pushed up close to my body. It slides in ridiculously easily and I glimpse his eyes widen with momentary surprise then slit with pain as he releases me and staggers back, clutching his side. Blood seeps shockingly fast through the thin cotton shirt. He sways and falls.

Soundlessly I turn and look up the empty street. I can't believe what is happening and stare back down at the crumpled shape now lying slumped under the laburnum tree. Its yellow swags of flowers dip gracefully over the boy's body and gently sweep the red tassel of the scabbard merging in a growing pool of blood nearby.

I turn rigidly and walk up the alley, straight into the busy Dongsanhuah Road. Bearing right to the hotel, I resist turning back for one last horrified look.

The coach has arrived and drifts of tourists are leaving the Landmark's foyer. Mechanically I approach Rob standing by the bus anxiously peering up the road for me. I feel numb but curiously in control.

'Oh there you are,' he says, relief in his voice. 'Did you get it?'

No *he* did, I think grimly and then aloud: 'None left. Doesn't matter,' and disappear into the anonymity of the bus. I slip into a window seat and turn my face outwards though I can see the reflection of the others climbing in, laughing and chatting - mates for life after five days together in an alien world - swinging cameras, bags and cold-pressed orchids in cellophane up into the luggage racks. The doors slide closed and the driver starts up. Our tour guide hangs grinning over the front seats. He's been pretty guarded, only partially communicative up to now, selling the party line to over-inquisitive Brits, but now his fine-boned sallow face crinkles in smiles, anticipating tips, hopefully dollars.

I let the talk and banter drift over me and as the bus pulls out of the hotel parking bay, stare at the milling multitudes outside. We gather speed lurching into the swollen river of bicycles, taxis, donkeys, more bicycles, dormobiles, trishaws, yet more bicycles.

Passing an alley in the Beijing dusk I can just make out, up the darkening road, a huddle of people gathered excitedly under a laburnum tree whose golden blossoms glow and quiver in the fading evening light.

THE FACE OF TRUTH

Ann Bryce

The woman at the supermarket check-out glanced at her watch in annoyance.

'It's always the same,' she remarked to the customer standing behind her. 'They always change the roll at the till I use. It's so irritating!'

The customer behind her pretended not to hear, wary of being led into a rude dialogue. But the woman would not give up.

'I deliberately chose this check-out because the queue was the smallest!' She was almost shouting now. 'It seems once again I have been thwarted!'

The girl on the cash register looked embarrassed and was all fingers and thumbs trying to replace the roll.

'Do hurry up, young lady,' snapped the woman. 'I really haven't got all day!'

The customer behind muttered something about having forgotten to buy her cornflakes and hurried back to the shelves. By now the girl had managed to get back into business.

'About time too,' muttered the woman between her teeth, now packing her groceries with the determined ferocity of a stalking lion. Minutes later she staggered heavily laden from the store, but smiling. A stupid little school leaver in a down-town, shoddy supermarket was not going to spoil her afternoon. Oh no! In one of her carrier bags lay her treat, most carefully wedged between the toilet rolls and the sliced loaf. Her kiwi fruit flan! Just what she fancied! A bit extravagant, perhaps, but didn't she deserve it? She earned it after all.

Sylvia Wade was a most self-contained person. She had never married; never wanted to. She neither borrowed nor loaned; had an easy job which gave her reasonable satisfaction in the civil service and which provided her with an adequate income. She lived alone in a neat, though not ostentatious, ground floor flat in the suburbs of Birmingham and treated herself to the cinema once a week. Life was pleasant and full, she had good neighbours, needed nothing, enjoyed her privacy, attended

Church regularly every Sunday and of course, looked after Tigger her cat.

As she fixed the key into her front door lock she noticed that the curtains were not quite as white as she would have liked.
'Must steep those again,' she thought. 'Never know who might come.'
The trouble was, nobody ever did. She opened the door and rushed along the hall into the tiny kitchen almost throwing the carrier bags onto the table in her haste not to drop them. Her haste got the better of her, however, because Tigger happened to run under her feet at the same time. One bag managed successfully to land but the other caught the edge of the table, spewing its contents like a man who had just realised he had had too much to drink.

'Oh damn!' Sylvia exclaimed. 'Tigger, I'll . . .!'
She grovelled about the floor scooping up satsumas which were now, unfortunately, sticky with kiwi fruit juice. 'It's all that stupid girl's fault,' she moaned. 'If she hadn't botched up the money roll I'd have got home sooner and this wouldn't have happened.'

She managed to salvage more than half of the flan and then carefully washed the floor. Then she put the kettle on and busied herself opening a tin of cat food and preparing herself some spaghetti on toast. She sat down to eat, staring with pleasure at the remains of her kiwi fruit flan which held pride of place in the centre of the table. Life was good, She could take care of herself and afford the odd pleasure now and again. Tigger purred.

It was while she was washing up that she first became conscious of a low, moaning noise. She stopped clattering the crocks with her hands immersed in mountains of suds, her head tilted a little to one side like a worried cocker spaniel.

'Funny,' she said to herself. 'Wonder what that was.' Hearing nothing more she finished her chores and wandered into the small sitting room where the rays of the evening sun spattered the green carpet with golden shadows.
'Just catch the news,' she thought. 'See what's going on in the world.'
She bent down to put the plug in and again became aware of that low, moaning, disturbing sound.

'Where's it coming from?' she wondered. 'Perhaps it's Sheila next door or her baby, or something. Better go see.'

She allowed the telly plug to drop noiselessly to the floor. Two minutes later, Sheila Harrington who occupied the flat next to Sylvia, stared at her in surprise.

'Someone crying?' she asked.

'No, it's not me and the baby's asleep. Wonder who it could be? Crying did you say?'

'Well, more like moaning; a distressed sound. Might be from Jim upstairs. Sometimes I can hear him. I'll just nip up and check he's all right.'

Sylvia climbed sharply up the glistening, grey, mock-granite stairs to door number three. There was no reply to her knock. There was no sound from within even with her ear pressed close to the key hole. Retracing her steps she thought she must have imagined the whole thing but half-way down she heard the sound again. She began to feel slightly alarmed. It had to be coming from somewhere, but where? Returning home she plugged in the TV, saw the remainder of the news, made herself a cup of coffee, listened to her favourite CD - The Blues Brothers singing 'Everybody Needs Someone', read a little Stephen King, enjoyed a twenty minute nap, let the cat out, locked up and decided to go to bed.

She loved her bedroom. It was decorated in pink wallpaper sprinkled with a profusion of tiny red and white flowers. The frilled curtains matched, as did the duvet cover, headboard, lampshades, waste bin and bedside tablecloth. Sylvia had taken great pains to make this room ultra-feminine and pretty. The dressing table was kidney-shaped with a beautiful oval mirror, gilt-edged. She sat down on the padded pink stool and gazed happily at herself. As she looked, once again she became aware of the moaning, only this time it was clearer and louder. It seemed almost to come from within the mirror itself. Her smile froze for an instant, then imperceptibly disappeared altogether. Her mouth drooped at the corners as sadly as a tulip's petal in a central heated room. Tears began to well in her eyes. Her lips quivered as from behind them, came the moan.

In her self-sufficiency, Sylvia thought she had overcome what it felt like to be lonely. The moan became a shriek, a scream. The tears billowed into torrents. Uncontrollable sobs wracked her self-sufficient body until it crumbled into helplessness. In her wild despair she sent the pretty table lamp reeling; smashed her dainty crystal vase; flung crochet mats in confusion on the floor; clasped the wallpaper breaking her finely chiselled nails. Her well-groomed hair raged like tangled twigs at the zenith of a storm. All hell broke loose from within the confines of her once safe self. She gripped the mirror between white-clenched fists and glared in awful disbelief at her deeply anguished face. The mirror cracked.

KNIFEPOINT
Kate Johnson

I was glad he was dead.

It had been a very brief struggle, I was surprised that it was over so quickly. A little disappointed too. There was a sort of perverse delight to be had from these sorts of things. The longer you fought, the better victor you were.

He shouldn't have tried to fight back. Didn't he know who I was? Didn't he see the gun?

The look on his face when it went off. Horror. Shock. Pain. For a moment I thought I was in trouble there, but it was worth it for the cash I gained.

I counted the roll of notes in my hand. Most satisfactory. And the credit cards too. Of course, they wouldn't be useful for very long. Only until someone found out that he was dead, because whoever heard of a dead person using a credit card? Maybe I should check the body for jewellery.

I peeked out from my hiding place around the corner. It was so dark. There were only a few meagre, useless sodium bulbs and they cast more shadows than light. I could see the body on the glistening road, blood beginning to ooze around him, making pretty Rorschach patterns on the tarmac. That'll teach him to wander around here late at night. Unarmed. Lots of money on him. Stupid man.

I felt for the ring on my finger. Where was it? It wasn't there!
He must have pinched it!

The thought that perhaps it had rolled away occurred to me but I preferred to imagine that he had taken it. He thought he might be able to light-finger me, is that it? Well then, he deserved to die. Stupid man, Stupid.

Checking around to see that no one was there, I slid around the corner, silent as a shadow. I am a genius at this sort of thing. So quick, so silent. They'll never catch me. I ran noiselessly across to the cover of the next building, but a sudden shout caught my attention.

Melting back into the shadows I pressed myself against the dark wall and waited. They hadn't seen me.

I told you I'd never get caught.

Damn! Two men and a woman, probably trying to put in some extra time and gain some Brownie points with their boss, had exited one of the industrial buildings, headed towards the car park and spotted my man.

My first thought was that they'd fleece him before I could get there. My hard-earned (well, quickly fought-for) prize was going to be whipped away from me before I could get to it. And my ring too! The bastard stole my ring. Well, he won't get to keep it. I still have my gun. I can polish them off, too. You wait and see if I don't.

I crept towards the edge of the light, where the shadow was deepest and felt for the pistol.

Where is it? I can't find it. It's not in its holster. Where is it? My gun! I need my gun!

Panicking now, I could do little but watch as the woman picked it up off the bloody ground and screeched in terror.
'Is he dead?' she whimpered.

The men were kneeling down, feeling for a pulse. Of course he's dead, you idiots. Now go away and leave me to collect my loot. I'm the victor. Battle rules dictate that I should get whatever I want of the dead man's possessions. The fact that I attacked him with that very purpose in mind serves only to underline my point, I think. It's easier to rob someone when they're not alive to resist. Although I have to say, he didn't put up much of a fight.

There's my ring. There, on the floor. Glinting in the orange sodium light. Wouldn't it be funny if they tried to use it to identify the body? Wouldn't it be hilarious if they though *I* was dead?

They were going through his wallet now. Well, tough, I thought, I've got all the goodies already. Unless you can find a use for his loyalty cards and a driving license, I really don't think you'll find -

But wait a minute. That's *my* wallet! Those are pictures of *my* family they're pawing over!

That's my address they're reading out from the driving licence. My description they are giving to the police on their poncey mobile phones.

It *had* been a very brief struggle. No wonder I was surprised it was over so quickly. No wonder I was disappointed.

He shouldn't have tried to fight back. Didn't he know who I was? Didn't he see the gun?

The look on his face when it went off. Horror. Shock. Pain. My pain. Who was it pointing at? For a moment I thought I was in trouble there.

For a moment, I was right.

THE PARK BENCH
Stephen Hullyer

What it was that made Peter stop at the park bench, he didn't know. He sat down gratefully and wondered what changes this park bench must have seen. If it had a mouth the stories would be truly captivating.

Suddenly a delicious aroma floated under his nose. He sniffed but couldn't quite make out where it was coming from. There was no description he could give to it. The nearest adjective would be fresh flowers. He turned his head in its direction and he just caught the end of a whispered conversation. '. . .OK we'll make it Tuesday . . . 10am . . .'

He still couldn't make out where the voices were coming from but he was intrigued. The aroma suggested it was perfume, that meant a woman, but he'd only heard one voice and that was definitely a man! And what about Tuesday at 10am? Was it an appointment? A meeting? And where?

Peter didn't know the answers but a gut feeling told him something was wrong. Of course, it might have been a mother and son discussing a confidential meeting, but somehow, he doubted it.

It was Friday today. So he had four days. Peter got up and walked across the park towards the shops. He joined the busy street and watched as everyone passed him by. Every shop was a possible target and then he heard the unmistakable sound of someone keying in their four-digit code. A bank! That was it! There was only one bank in the town and it was going to be raided at 10am on Tuesday! He assumed it was this Tuesday and, even if it were, what could he do? If he told anyone that the bank was going to be hit no one would believe him but maybe the police would.

He walked over to the police station where he asked to see the duty officer. After a brief wait the officer came out. 'Now, I understand you have some information for me,' he said.
'About a robbery. When did this happen?'
'It hasn't, not yet anyway.' Peter said.
'Well, if it hasn't. Then I don't understand.' The duty officer's tone had changed to one of suspicion.

'How do you know about a robbery? Are you part of it?'

'No, but I overhead a conversation about 10am on Tuesday. From where I was sitting the only significant place of importance is the bank.'

The duty officer laughed. 'Thank you for your information, sir. But I think you're wide of the mark. That conversation could have been anything from an appointment to a bus timetable.'
'I considered that, Peter said, sensing where the conversation was going. 'But, you have to admit, I might be right.'
'Sir,' repeated the duty officer, showing Peter the door.
'Most of our time is spent following up leads. They nearly always are dead ends. As I feel this is. Goodbye.'

Peter left forlornly. If the police wouldn't believe him there was no way the bank would. His only chancc lay in letting the raid happen and suffering the consequences.

Tuesday came. Peter didn't know if he was pleased or not. If the raid was to be today then he was determined to be there. He asked someone the time. It was nine-fifty. He entered the bank and pretended to leaf through the various leaflets that advertised the different services. The door opened and in walked a man who banged a case down on the counter. It was the guard from the truck. No sooner had he put the case down the door burst open.

'Everyone on the floor,' yelled a man. 'We don't want any dead heroes, do we?'

The voice was muffled as if the man was wearing a mask. Peter strained his ears but couldn't make out if that was the voice he'd heard in the park.

As Peter dropped to the ground that special aroma came to his nose again. He smiled ironically to himself. From his position he could tell that there were only two people involved in the raid. One was obviously taking the money while the other was crowd control.

Thankfully the incident was over quickly. Peter was questioned all day as the evidence against him mounted. Eventually, he was allowed to go home. That night, as he listened to the TV, the manager of the bank gave a personal plea for any information, concerning the raid. Peter couldn't believe it. There was no mistaking it. That was the voice he'd heard in the park. His first clue.

The next day Peter returned to the police and told them who the voice belonged to. At first they were sceptical but then it all began to fit into place. They arrested the bank manager who confessed to the crime.

'This has been the easy bit,' the police said. 'Catching the other member would be harder.'
'I could spot her,' Peter said confidently. 'Close up.'
'Her? You think it's a woman?'
'Of course,' said Peter, trying to surpass a grin. 'How many blokes do you know who wear perfume?'

The bank manager admitted to having an accomplice. She was a secretary in an office, across the road from the bank. A line-up was arranged. Peter slowly walked along the line, looking at the faces and then he smelt the perfume. He stopped in front of the woman and touched her on the shoulder.
'This one,' he said proudly.

As she was led away she turned to Peter and asked. 'How did you know it was me? We were both wearing masks.'
'Your perfume,' Peter said. 'It smells like fresh flowers. I smelt it in the park and again in the bank during the raid.'
'That was a present, from Mike, the bank manager,' she said softly, realising how she'd been caught.

The same duty officer said to Peter, 'If she hadn't have worn that perfume and, if you hadn't have sat on that park bench, you would never have known, would you?'
'Oh, I don't know,' Peter said, smiling. 'It's amazing how powerful your senses become when you're blind!'

TEMPTING FATE
Susan Roberts

No, he didn't want a Chinese replica of a Swiss army knife. How reliable would that be, he wondered sarcastically, if you were stuck up a mountain in dire need of a corkscrew. He didn't need a hideous plastic Dalmatian dog that went woof-woof to delight visitors as they came up the garden path. For God's sake, who were these people that were sending an invitation to sample free pairs of tights to a Mr Daniel Swallow. He could do without the hundred and fifty assorted bulbs for the garden and the ghastly plastic gnome that came with them. The Yes/No envelope from Readers Digest provoked the most disgust and he gathered up all the mail to sling it in the bin. It was all junk, rubbish and psychological sneakiness to get you to buy a load of stuff you thought you couldn't live without. And he should know, he had been Fab-Adds top marketing man for the previous six months. You couldn't sell anything to Daniel Swallow unless he couldn't live without it.

The gypsy selling pegs at the front door had fooled him. Where there should have been an old crone wearing big earrings, a flamboyant skirt and triangular headscarf there was a slightly dowdy and suburban woman. Indeed, when he answered the door he thought he was going to get quizzed by neighbourhood watch or bored to death by a local parish councillor. Would he buy some pegs from a gypsy, the woman wanted to know. No, he bloody well wouldn't he thought, eyeing her ordinary suit and slight unsensible shoes and feeling irritated that he had been conned.

'I don't need any pegs thank you,' he said briskly. Her smile was polite, but something in her eyes made him want to cross his fingers behind his back. This irritated him even more.
'I'm sorry to have troubled you sir,' said the woman and walked off, leaving Daniel to feel annoyed and frustrated with everyone and everything for the rest of the day.

Later on, Daniel would often think about that meeting and wish he had never answered the door. For someone who made it his business never to stop and consider anything too deeply, this was as much as Daniel was prepared to think. If someone had told Dan, (as they often told each other), that he always paddled at the shallow end of warmth and sincerity towards his fellow human beings, he would never listen. Just buy some pegs, spend a tiny amount of cash, have a chat about the weather, wave her cheerily on her way, were not pieces of advice that Daniel would take kindly to. Daniel was terrified of mellow moments, scared of the dark and completely impervious to any human agency that tried to alter his course. What Dan needed was a supernatural intervention. Fate was duly summoned. Fate always relished the chance to take someone on a spiritual journey. As with every true course of destiny, it was up to Dan whether he got on the bus or not.

It was shortly after the meeting with the gypsy that Daniel Swallow became cursed by a small, white, Fiat Panda. What began as small incidents of petty inconvenience and frustration soon escalated into a downward spiralling, sweaty terror. The scariest thing of all, for Daniel Swallow, was that he began to lose money.

Fate considered the importance of cash to Daniel Swallow. The profile of a man in Marketing, driving a Ford Mondeo up and down a lot of stressful motorways with his jacket swinging from a hanger in the back, playing squash, decking himself out like a walking label and collecting gadgets because he experienced panic attacks if he didn't have them, meant that losing money was likely to disturb more than just his peaceful state of expendable income.

Instead of dreaming of Ralph Loren, Timberland watches and Gucci loafers, cashmere sweaters and a nifty little clock/calculator finished in brushed chrome that could tell him the time in every world zone, Daniel began to have nightmares about a car. In the dream, the car stopped in front of him and the gypsy got out. She was menacing and frighteningly focused as she walked towards him, her hand outstretched and demanding her peg money. The nightmare happened every night and after three weeks Daniel had developed a twitch. The night terrors were only surpassed by the ones that happened during the day. Daniel was in serious trouble. He whipped out his calculator and calculated.

In the last sixty-five days he had been late for work seventeen times. This meant that he had lost his good time keeping bonus, which amounted to ten percent of his daily salary. In sixty-five days Daniel had lost £784.25 and all because of a Fiat Panda. He was cursed, although fate did not expect this fact to impinge on his consciousness just yet. Daniel did what he always did in any scary situation. He put his head down, switched on the auto-pilot and just kept going.

The car from hell waited for him every morning. He was slowly coming to know this as a truth. He had started to spend hours pouring over street maps in an effort to outwit it, but whichever way he tried to sneak through the streets and get onto the main road, the Fiat would hove into view two or three cars ahead of him, then wreak its malevolent havoc. His had been a slow awakening to this mechanical horror that now stalked him every day.

At first it had just broken down. Regularly. It had two punctures. One day it ran over a shopping trolley. On three occasions the exhaust had collapsed onto the tarmac, sending up showers of sparks and making a fearful grinding noise. Whatever street the car chose for operation grid-lock, it showed great cunning and tactical skill. That particular street was always narrow with parked cars. Everything came to a grinding halt. People got out of their vehicles, had a fag, chatted, then pushed the car to some vacant spot which was usually three hundred yards further up the road.

An old lady drove the car. In Daniel's increasingly weird world of persecution and paranoia, the old lady became the gypsy's accomplice, sent forth to get him. Dan would sit in his car and alternate between rage and a strange paranormal fear. He himself could not get out of his car and throttle her, but he could not understand why no one else did. The more it happened and the more these amiable idiots pushed her car up and down every side street on the map, the more unnerved he became.

As if to taunt him even more, things began to appear on the roof of the car, left there by their fiendishly-minded occupant. He watched her sewing basket get crushed and something undefinable in a butcher's bag get squashed by a motorised disability scooter. One day she drove along with a frying pan on top until it slid off and went under the wheels of a motorbike. Daniel was so late for work that day (because of the ambulance!) he missed the presentation for 'Pegsons' Premier Pet Foods'; his marketing project which had promised so much in the way of back slaps, power and prestige in the design and labelling department and an upgrade for the Mondeo. He felt he truly understood what the term 'gutted' meant. He decided he had to do something. Fate, who had been keeping an eye on the proceedings, watched with a dispassionate interest to see what Daniel would do. What fate witnessed was the shot fired in the dark by the desperate who have nothing to lose.

Miss Swift was never aware of a lot of chaos in her life, but if she had ever looked behind her she might have been. As she drove her treasured Fiat through the driving rain, heading towards the chemist to pick up her prescription, the front of her car rocking with its huge window screen wipers going at super-fast speed gave the impression that she was driving some kind of strange hovercraft that was battling out the elements on a violent sea. At least that was what it looked like to Daniel Swallow as he loomed into her limited swathe of vision, just as one of her wipers detached itself and shot off somewhere into the torrential rain. Oh dear, thought Miss Swift, slamming on the brakes, but then she breathed a sigh of relief as she realised the sudden blurring of her vision had been an act of mechanical failure and not her cataracts finally getting the better of her.

Daniel loomed larger and wetter against the drivers' window, looking himself as if he had been blown off course. While Miss Swift considered if he wanted to hijack her car or return her lost wiper blade, Daniel pressed an envelope against the wet glass and gestured wildly for her to wind down the window. Curious as to what was going on, Miss Swift tentatively lowered a letterbox worth of glass but before she had chance to speak the soaking figure outside had thrust the envelope through the window, then disappeared into the hammering rain.

It took a lot to rattle Miss Swift, she was used to 'things' happening around her. She parked the car outside the chemist with her usual unflappable precision and read the letter while she waited for her eye medication. It read:
'Dear Madam,
I would very much like to buy your Fiat. This is not a joke. I am a member of the Fiat Appreciation Society. Your car would be treasured and restored to its original showroom condition. To show you I am sincere, I have enclosed a cheque for £1000. Once again, I must assure you that my offer is totally genuine. You can contact me at any time at the number/address written below.

Respectfully
Daniel Swallow'

Well, thought Miss Swift. How fortuitous. All this happening the day after the doctor had told her she could not drive her little Fiat any more. Her eyesight was deteriorating, Doctor Heath had said and she would soon become a danger to the public. If only he knew.

While Miss Swift read her letter, Daniel went home and sat and waited. He did not have to wait long. Miss Swift considered the cheque and the strange man's letter. She decided that someone must have answered her prayers. She phoned him and agreed to his very generous offer.

Daniel did not feel the ecstatic burst of emotion he expected. Instead he felt a slow kind of relief seeping into his body and a sense that somewhere wheels were turning within wheels that were somehow going to rebalance the set of horrible events that were still waiting somewhere in his future. He had great hopes that the nightmares would subside and that normal life would resume, once he had got his hands on that car. He took possession of Ethel (of course, that car would have a name) and felt much the same way he always felt when he had won and got what he wanted.

He quietly took Ethel to a scrap yard and got £25 for her. Although it grieved him sorely, he put the money into a charity box and hoped he would rid himself of the taint of guilt he felt as he remembered the face of Miss Swift, wiping a tear from her eyes as she said goodbye to dear Ethel. Any feelings of unease did not last long and while Ethel was busy being made into a small cube of metal, Daniel began to consider, not too deeply, the risk factors in saying 'no' to gypsies, tinkers and other itinerant sales people. He thought grudgingly that they had a good marketing strategy and he only wished he could use curses in his own line of work. He began to formulate an idea involving a Good Luck/Bad Luck envelope and wondered if he could possibly sell it. Fate meanwhile, was considering what to do about Daniel and decided that Ethel should not have been cubed in vain.

Several days later when Daniel returned home from work, he found his own Good Luck/Bad Luck envelope waiting for him on the doormat. He opened it and read:

Dear Mr Swallow

I am writing to you to thank you so much for your generous cheque. I hope that you and Ethel are getting along. It would be nice to see her one day when you have restored her. I just wanted to let you know that the money you gave me has helped me a lot. I put it towards having eye surgery and I have had my cataracts removed. The operation was so successful I have been told that I can drive a car again. I have just bought another Fiat. Thank you once again for your wonderful generosity.

Yours sincerely

Doris Swift

THE CALL OF CHILDHOOD
Lynda Holt

I stood at the entrance to the house and watched as the old man slowly closed the door. Stunned into physical immobility, my thoughts exploded with incomprehension. Numbed with confusion, I made a vain attempt to rationalise what I had just been told by beginning a mental re-appraisal of the past.

My life had been one of inconsistency, sadness, trauma and despair, but paradoxically my childhood had been a delight. The first eleven years had been spent in idyllic happiness, free from the cares and pressures of an extraordinarily difficult adulthood. During the summer months, the sun had shimmered on the brook and myself and many friends had paddled in its cool, clear water. We built innumerable dams, constructed out of fallen trees and small rocks intertwined with willow sticks. When our attempts to slow the current of the water were successful, we would submerge our small hot bodies in the deeper water. The winters would encompass the pleasures of Bonfire Night when we wrote our names in the sky with sparklers and ate home-made treacle toffee whilst watching the night sky sing with explosions of colour. This event foreshadowed the snow filled winter when the sledges would be in constant use on the surrounding hills in which our small Lancastrian town nestled.

I was surrounded by love, both sets of grandparents lived within walking distance of our house, as did numerous aunts and uncles. I was Daddy's little girl, had a wide array of friends and was successful at school. Each year myself and Colin Matthews would vie for the top of the class position, it was an annual two horse race. At eleven years old I passed my eleven plus examination and attended the local grammar school; my happiness knew no bounds.

In retrospect it was an event that occurred at this time, shortly before my twelfth birthday, which spun my life into the path of oncoming disaster, an alternative life route to despair. The predicted straight line of happiness, joy and contentment transmogrified into a tangent of alternative existence; one of trauma and sadness. It appeared to be an iniquitous event at the time, we simply moved house; an event which most people undertake at some point. In our case however, it was not that simple as the house to which we went was three hundred and fifty miles away. Gone were the black earth and rolling hills of Lancashire, the dry, sandy, flat landscape of Suffolk became my world. It was a world in which I existed in a form of alienation, my broad Lancashire vowels giving rise to endless amusement among my peers. Gone was the grammar school which was situated within walking distance of home; a daily twenty mile, one and a half hour bus journey preceded the attendance of Mills Grammar School. An educational establishment attended by wealthy elitist boarders together with a select number of day girls; no room for the working class hoi-polloi in this school.

From that time onwards my life followed a reasonable predictable course, although the periods of longing for my grandparents and my home town intensified rather than diminished. Spasmodic episodes of total loneliness began to dog my existence, it was a pattern which was to be repeated for the next forty years. Repetitious house moves ensured no consistency with regard to lasting friendships. My eighteen-year marriage ended in divorce and although I met someone else to whom I became engaged, he departed to pastures new after a lengthy affair. Best friends have fallen by the wayside, my grandparents died many years ago. At seventeen years of age my parents decided to move away, taking my two younger brothers with them. A feeling of complete and utter loneliness fills my existence. All that keeps me company is the intense effort of repeatedly attempting to build a new life for myself, an effort which becomes more strenuous as the years pass.

I try to be philosophical about the hardships I have undergone, after all there are few people who have not suffered and overcome some form of adversity. However, no matter how I try to justify the events of my life, I cannot equate the amount of unhappiness which has been dealt to me with any rationality. I have behaved no worse than anyone else apart from one unfortunate incident but isn't everyone allowed one mistake? Nobody's perfect and for that one error, I sincerely paid the price. In short my life would be a standing joke if it were not for the fact that its catalogue of disasters is too painful to make light of. The devil on my shoulder sits and waits until life is running fairly smoothly before deciding to intervene.

How do I cope? I retreat to my childhood; to those glorious eleven years in which happiness permeated every waking hour. I visit the house of my childhood in my dreams and travel through the rooms, recalling the gloriously joyful atmosphere which existed there. I wander into my bedroom and watch myself trying to stay awake, waiting for Father Christmas to come, watching the night sky for a glimpse of his sleigh. I open the door of the bathroom and look at the wallpaper there, alive with beautiful fish of myriad hues which swim ceaselessly on a bright blue liquid background. I see the pattern of the linoleum on the floor, the mock parquet flooring effect through which I would invent stepping stones on which to cross the bathroom. On into my parents' bedroom, I see the pink music box with the dancing fairy on the top and listen to its haunting clockwork melody. I happen upon my brother's bedroom in which we stood, faces pressed to the window, watching the dying embers of the bonfire each year. I see the picture of Jesus hanging on the wall above the bookcase; and the tiny pink roses on the wallpaper. Strolling down the stairs, I recall falling down them head over heels until landing unceremoniously in a collision with the cupboard in the hallway. The gas meter lived in here, an implement of wonder to me as it had to be fed an unremitting diet of shiny silver shillings. From the hallway, I open the door to the living room. The fish tank stands in the corner, the sound of the air filter murmuring softly in the background. In the opposite corner stands the piano, its lid opened and the Skater's Waltz music sheet open upon its stand. The huge green sofa squats comfortably in front of the coal fire into whose flames I stare and create imaginary scenes of red and yellow hues. The dining table stands folded by the window, sadly bereft without its display of appetising food and without the five of us sat around it chatting happily throughout the meal. I leave the living room and venture into the kitchen; there on the ceiling is the Victorian washing rack from which the laundry hung each Monday smelling of starch and pristinely whitened with Dolly Blue. The new washing machine sits gleaming beneath the window; the first one my mother has ever owned. There in the corner is the pantry door, I do not need to open it for I know what lies beyond. The first words that I could ever write at four years old were the ubiquitous 'Nip is a dog'. Nip was destined to be reproduced, along with a simple angular drawing of him on any flat surface. The pantry walls proved ideal for this purpose and in the pantry Nips cavort and dance in an eternal montage. The kitchenette, white and yellow sits above the hatch cover set in the wooden floor, to me a portal to another world; but to my father merely the house foundations. Infrequently my father and I would venture into this strange underworld, the smell of the dry dust and the eerie silence was both oppressive and intensely exciting. After leaving the kitchen, I enter the back hallway, there my home-made toy cupboard filled with a child's delight sits in the corner. On the window sill nearby sits a jam jar brimming with soon to hatch frogspawn. The coal cupboard is to my left, the smell of the coal dust redolent of freshly dug earth. Finally I take my leave through the stout, wooden back door, a door which I once proudly exclaimed to my father could stop elephants. 'There aren't many elephants in Lancashire pet,' he whispered with a smile on his face.

Many times I visit my childhood home, both waking and sleeping, imagining and dreaming. Within my dreams, my grandparents live again, as do my childhood friends, Father Christmas, fairies and elves and everything that is pure and wholesome. My childhood was a time to which I long to return and on some form of subconscious level I am acutely aware that the emotions of childhood are intertwined with those of death. For this reason, death holds no fear, but promises a welcoming release and a possible gateway to a joyful existence.

I have reached middle age, but it is as if I have awakened to find that my life has passed without me being fully aware of it. The years between my childhood and the present appears ethereal and ephemeral, totally dissimilar to the emotional intensity of my childhood. I have become aware of my own mortality and feel its welcoming touch caressing me. A message appears to accompany the understanding, that it will soon be too late. Too late for what I wonder? Then the realisation; I must visit my childhood home instead of relying on dreams and memory. I must physically walk through those rooms where my happiness knew no bounds and relive my memories.

I travel to my childhood town, slowly drive to the front of my former home where I park by the lamp post to which our skipping ropes used to be tied. An explosion of memories assails my mind. After several tentative attempts, I finally gather enough courage to knock on the door. An elderly man opens the door, his rheumy eyes fixed on mine as if drawn there by some primordial knowledge.

'I'm sorry to trouble you, but this house was my home for the first eleven years of my life. I know that it's a terrible imposition, but it would mean so much to me if I could just have one last look around it.'

'You wouldn't want to come inside,' he said, never taking his eyes from mine for one second.

'Why ever not?' I asked.

'Because this house is haunted.'

'Haunted? Haunted by whom?'

'By you,' he said as he began to slowly close the door.

SHE SLEEPS BETTER NOW
Terence L Baldwin

'Right Mrs Templeton. Sorry to keep you waiting. If you would read the typed statement and sign it you are free to go,' said the woman police constable. She placed a sheet of typewritten paper on the table.

Carol Templeton nodded. It wasn't the whole truth but as much as she was prepared to tell. She picked it up and commenced to read.

I was picking roses in my garden. I heard a squeal of tyres and then a crash. My initial reaction was to rush indoors and telephone the Fire Brigade. I had taken a couple of steps when I heard a scream. It made me jump. I could see a van see-sawing wildly on the edge of the old quarry.

Suddenly there was another scream, followed by several loud curses. I dropped my roses and hurried to the rear of the van to stop its movement. The handle of the door turned easily and I pulled it open. 'Don't move,' I called out. 'I . . . I'll get help.'
'Thank buggery someone's there,' the driver said.

Carol's mind drifted back in time. For some reason the dark silhouette against the windscreen had troubled her and a prickling sensation had tumbled over her entire body. She shuddered before reading on.

I must have released my hold on the van because it tilted upwards. That's when the man yelled . . . 'Hey, what the bloody hell is happening? Just take it easy and do as I tell you.'
I asked if he was hurt and told him not to make any severe movements.

The man twisted towards me. 'I think I've broken my leg. Every time I move it's bloody agony. You'll have to help me. I'll tell you what to do,' he replied.

I didn't like his arrogant manner and I guess I released my hold on the van again. 'I'll call the Fire Brigade,' I said.

The tail end of the van lifted and he shouted, 'No, don't leave me. You bloody stupid or something. You'll have to climb in and help me.'

Carol rubbed her eyes. She remembered at the time there had been something in his voice, some tone or inflection which had brushed against the curtains of her memory. Unwanted images had struggled to emerge against the fragile defences she had painfully erected.

She continued reading.

I must have hesitated because he shouted at me. 'What's the matter with you woman? Why the hell are you still out there? This bloody thing could go any minute. Get in and help me out of this seat.'

'Wouldn't it be safer if I stopped it from rocking while you got yourself out,' I asked.

'Haven't you been bloody listening to me. I'm sure my right leg is broken. I need help. Once in the passenger seat I can lower the back and you can pull me out. The quicker you damn well get in here the sooner I'll be out of danger won't I,' he rasped, his tone condescending, as if talking to a child.

I was grateful I had changed out of my skirt and into jeans.

'I'm coming. Stay as still as you can,' I said.

Slowly I inched my way on hands and knees into the dark interior. I really didn't enjoy that very much. The floor became steeper as I moved deeper into the van's interior. Any attempt on my part to move quickly resulted in the vehicle rocking wildly.

I stretched forward another couple of inches. A sharp pain shot up my leg as my knee came down onto something sharp. I cried out and flung myself backwards. The van bounced on its rear wheels and I heard small stones breaking away underneath. It was awful.

Carol stared at the paper she was holding. The words disappeared into oblivion and she allowed herself to be propelled into the past.

'Bloody hell. You'll have us over the edge you stupid tart,' the dark figure before her shouted.

She had frozen. Vague images pierced the curtains of her mind for a moment before her defences brushed them aside. You stupid tart . . . tart . . . tart, echoed over and over in her head. Sounds gradually merged and subsided and she saw herself in another place.

Twelve months ago she had been walking through a car park when someone had come up behind her and slipped a noose of thin cord round her neck.

In the gloom of the van Carol's fingers unconsciously went to her throat seeking the rope of nightmares. That incident had ripped away the reins of control she had over her existence. She was no longer able to stop the buffeting of fate as it swept her along the river of life.

'You bloody, stupid tart,' the voice shouted out of the darkness of the van's interior. 'What the hell's the matter with you. You gone ice on me or something. How many times do you need to be told?'

Carol shuddered and shrugged her defences into place. She stared intently at the man in the driving seat. His vague outline against the windscreen meant nothing to her. And yet it was disturbingly familiar.

She shook her head as if to clear her mind. So far so good she told herself as she continued reading.

After the van stopped rocking he sounded more anxious.
'Look, I haven't enough room to move this bloody leg,' he said. 'I'll have to open my door.'
I told him I didn't think that would be a good idea.
'Who cares what you think. I'm the one bloody trapped.'

In a sudden rush the door was wrenched from his hand and violently flung open. The balance of the van changed and it rocked dangerously. As the interior light swept away the darkness. I threw myself towards the rear and succeeded in restoring its stability.
'Bloody hell, I thought that was the end,' he said. 'I can see I'll have to do things myself.'

I balanced on my toes ready to adjust to the van's movement. Each movement he made brought a fresh stab of pain and shouted crudities.
'It's no use,' he gasped at last. 'You'll have to help me woman. Come on. Give me your bloody arm and look sharp about it,' he ordered.

I inched forward until I was close enough to touch him. By this time the driver had begun to panic as his frantic struggles to manoeuvre himself between the seats came to nothing. His hand shot out and fastened on my arm.

'For Christ sake do something.' he screamed. 'Before you kill both of us.'

In all statements there are certain things that cannot be told, Carol reflected. What happened next was one of them. She remembered turning as cold and rigid as stone. She could only stare at the hand which held her arm in its vice-like grip. The same tattoo of a skull and cross bones grinned evilly at her. The hand no longer grasped her arm but held 'the knife' . . . the knife that had glided over her skin.

The symbol of her nightmares shattered the defences she had built round her mind. 'It was you,' Carol hissed. 'You bastard,' she shouted, trying to pull herself away from the nightmare of nightmares.

'I don't know what you're talking about. Stop bloody jumping about woman,' he cried, panic crowding into his voice.

'You raped me you bastard. Because of you I've been unable to sleep or go out on my own,' Carol hissed. 'Because of you I lost my husband. Because of you I lost control over my life.'

'Look, I'm sorry, I don't . . . remember,' he blustered. 'Just help me out of here and I promise I'll do anything. Anything you ask.'

'Let me go. Let go of my arm,' Carol demanded. The loathing at his touch was quickly turning to black hatred.

His fingers tightened on her arm until they dug painfully into her flesh.

'Not until you bloody help me. If I go . . . you go with me . . . tart,' he snarled.

Carol winced at the word echoing in her mind before returning to her statement.

I was terrified his violent movements would cause the van to slip over the edge. I shouted at him to let me go but he only applied even more pressure. His grip on my arm was quite painful. I suppose I panicked. I bit him, wrenched myself free and stumbled to the rear.

Carol smiled to herself and looked out of the window. I wonder what they would do if they knew what had happened next, she thought. Carol believed that moment would be with her for the rest of her life. It was vivid in her memory.

Instead of scrambling out immediately Carol stopped. At that moment, realisation she was in control of her own, destiny struck her like a physical blow. She pondered the questions in her mind. Was he worth saving? Could she live with herself? A smile spread across her face.

She turned to look at the man who had defiled her body.
'Goodbye,' she said.

The coldness in her voice cut off the threat he was about to make.
'Hey, you can't leave me here. What do you think you're doing?'
It was the closest he had come to pleading.
With infinite care Carol balanced herself on the end of the van.
'When I'm fit I'll come looking for you . . . tart,' he hissed venomously.
'I'll enjoy you much more the second time.'

Without looking round or saying another word Carol used the tail end of the van as a diving board. The rear wheels hit the ground with a resounding thump. The van bounced high into the air and slithered forward taking the stones at the edge and the screams of its passenger with it as it slipped into empty space.

Carol picked up the pen and signed her statement with a flourish and handed it back. 'It was a complete shock. I never thought that would happen,' she said.

SWORD PLAY
Patricia Jeanne Hale

'By God, George, tis a filthy, raw, God-forsaken night.'

'Eh Tom, it be. I 'udn't be surprised if we 'ad a lot of cold weather ta come.'

'Well, we have entered the twentieth century now, George, and what do they say - *A new day, a new dawn.*'

'Dunno 'bout that, Tom, but reet now I could do with a good warm fire and something to warm the cockles of me heart! You got any dough, George?'

'Not a sausage, Tom, you knows I don't get paid till Friday night, and we owes last weeks and week afore that!'

'Oh well, let's walk round to the Old Belle Inn George, we might bump into Major Drummond, he usually treats the lads, if he's in a good mood. We could flatter him a little and in any case us can 'ave a good warm by fire!'

'That be a good idea Tom, we could ask 'im if 'ee believes in spirits.'

'Spect the only *spirits* he knows is what be in a glass George!'

'Well, let's go an' find out, Tom 'ang on, I'll just put me cloak on, looks like a wee drop of rain.'

''Tis quiet in town tonight, George, most of the population must be indoors I reckon, not much traffic about of any description.'

'Don't think I fancy goin' past Greyfriars Churchyard tonight, Tom, let's cut thru' the alley.'

'Y'know George, I don't agree with the Major, he says that 'the rumour has no foundation,' and truth is that in the 1300s a certain English Queen, Isabella, was buried at a spot in Greyfriars Churchyard. Her dying words were to have her dead husband's heart (whom she had murdered a few years previously, by the way), buried on her breast. And because her wish was not granted, she has haunted the Churchyard nightly every since. And will do so for evermore.'

'Well 'ee could be right, Tom, but I 'aint lived long enough to tell if 'tis truth, or no!'

They were often to be seen in the Old Belle Inn, for a get-together and a drink. The Old Major Drummond was a familiar figure at the quaint inn, and often bought a drink for the less well-off members of society.

London at the turn of the nineteenth century, with few cars and a prolific poor population. - Like Tom and George - Tom was convinced that a witch had been buried, quite by accident.

'Well.' said George, a tall fellow with a broad accent, well past his prime. 'Whichever it be, I 'udn't like to spend even a minute by yon gravestone, more'n my life's worth I tell 'ee.'

At the next table a young newspaper reporter, by the name of Oswald, was eagerly eavesdropping on the conversation. Then the door swung open, and in strode Major Drummond. He spoke with his loud deep voice. 'Filthy night outside tonight folks, looks like a storm is brewing!'

'Sir, may I take your cloak?' Shaking the cloak he carefully hung it on the peg by the shining sword hanging on the wall. 'My name is Oswald, Sir, I don't think I have the pleasure of making your acquaintance?' Thrusting his hand out to the old Major.

'My dear boy, everyone knows me for miles around!'

'Sir, I am very interested in the spirit reputed to haunt Greyfriars Churchyard after 12 pm midnight,' Oswald excitedly exclaimed.

'Another well known fact, but which I doubt, me boy,' said Major Drummond. 'The origin of the story has been distorted over the years, but she leaves the grave each night and no one would dare to enter the churchyard.'

By this time an eager group of listeners had gathered and were nodding in agreement.

'Have a drink young man!' Major Drummond waved to the landlord. 'Two tankards of the best you can brew!'

Sitting in the corner, his eyes rolling and lips turned up at the corners, in a sort of inane grin. His cap pulled well forward almost touching the empty pipe in his mouth, Tobias had lost his hair and teeth prematurely. In fact he looked much older than his 38 years. With a large family to support, times were hard.

'Come and wet your whistle with a wee drop of this, Tobias.'

George didn't like to see a man without a drink and a smoke.

Pouring half his ale into another glass. Tobias hastily joined the group around the Major's table.

They were a contrasting group - George unshaven and anxious to please everyone, with a heart of gold as broad as his accent. - Tom, being the referee type, so to speak. - Oswald the youngest of the group was beginning to get excited, no doubt from the unaccustomed tankard of ale! - And of course the wise old Major.

'Drink up folks, time's up!' came a voice from the bar.

'Good heavens, yes,' said Oswald. 'It's almost 11.30 pm and I haven't done my story yet.'

'What story is this?' enquired the Major.

'Well,' replied Oswald, 'I have to write an article each day for my paper and I've not done one today.'

'Would anyone volunteer to stay in Greyfriars Churchyard for the night? I will pay them 5 guineas if they stay on their own, and put a curse on the witch,' said the Major.

At this the Old Belle Inn became almost deserted, people muttering as they left; 'I'm not that hard up!'

Then a voice broke the silence. 'I'll do it! I'll stay on my own in the churchyard. I'm not frightened of any witch!' said Tobias, reaching up to take the long sword off the hook.

'You can have my cloak to keep you dry.' said Oswald.

Outside it was starting to rain heavily and a little crowd of onlookers were gathering round the porch, including Tom, George, and Major Drummond.

'It's almost 12.00 pm' said the Major. 'We'll escort you to the gates of the churchyard and leave you there.'

'If I see, or hear anything suspicious, I'll lay the ghost once and for all.' said Tobias waving the cutlass, glistening in the raindrops.

Hobnail boots clattering on the cobblestones, they set off for the churchyard gates. 'Got some nerve, that fellow,' said George.

'Oh, he'll do anything for a dare will Tobias,' replied a bystander.

'More like 'cos eeh needs the money,' replied George.

The rain had abated to a heavy drizzle as they arrived at the churchyard gates. It looked a grim and dismal place, in the light of a partly-hidden moon. The eerie silence was broken by the squeak and clatter of a chain, as they opened the old rusty gate. They all watched from behind the gates as Tobias bravely picked his way to the central grave and with sword in hand, and a wave in the direction of the others, he seated himself on top of the grave to await his vigil, and fulfil his promise to Oswald the newspaper man.

After several minutes the menfolk crowded outside the gates were getting a bit restless. Suddenly a piercing scream rent the atmosphere in two, like a knife. Tobias leapt to his feet, hands clenched high in the air, cutlass poised between. Simultaneously uttering the words; 'I curse thee,' and thrusting the sword with all his strength into the soft earth of the grave. Muttering words indistinguishable to the onlookers, he gave a couple more twists downwards to the handle, to make certain the sword had gone home.

Triumphantly throwing his arms in the air and uttering the words - 'The witch is dead - No! No! She's got me, she's on my back!' He collapsed in a crumpled heap over the grave. At this the reporter and witnesses outside the gate hurriedly ran for the safety of home in panic.

The next morning was dull and grey and the four men on returning to the graveside in the morning light - found the crumpled heap of Tobias still in the same position as they had last seen him, the night before. He was as grey as the gravestone and obviously had been dead for some time.

'Well,' said Major Drummond. 'We can't leave him here, come on lads, give us a hand, and we'll lift him onto this seat over here.'
The four of them bent over the thin body and gently took hold, two each end of him. But it was to no avail, try as they might they could not move him more than a few inches.

'That's funny,' said tom. 'It is almost as if the witch is still holding on to him.'

'Ah, wait a minute!' said George. 'Perhaps eeh's still 'oldin' onta sword. Let's look underneath.'
On closer examination the truth dawned on them.

On driving the cutlass with such force into the grave, Tobias had also pierced the back of the cloak he was wearing and about 12 inches of the cloak was still firmly embedded in the grave, along with the cutlass!

Poor Tobias, 'Died of a heart attack,' said the coroner.

'Apparently,' said the wise old Major, 'When Tobias jumped to his feet the cloak gripped him round the neck and shoulders, and he must have died of fright. What one might call, 'playing with a sword', no doubt!'
'Or 'witches' revenge',' remarked Tom.

'Aah wee'l, Oswald managed to get his story after all,' said George.'
'Yes,' said Oswald still trembling. 'When I can keep the pen still enough to write it down!'

'When you conclude your story my lad,' said the Major. 'Remember that anyone who goes hunting after midnight, can expect to encounter others on the prowl too, such as owls and, and . . .'
'Other beings?' suggested Tom.

THE MAN
Janette Anne Warwick

I lay on the bed in my usual place, not moving even an eyelid as the man charged into the bedroom. I heard him swearing under his breath as he dragged a bag from the top of the wardrobe and threw it on the bed - he missed me by inches but I stayed silent and unmoving as he pulled open drawers and began to put his clothes into the bag. All the time he was muttering and getting redder in the face, especially when he discovered the bag was almost full and he had more clothes to find room for. I felt sorrow as I saw him screw up the carefully ironed shirts and trousers into another small bag that he found in the bottom of the wardrobe as I thought of Annie's care when she had ironed them, she was always careful, so neat and clean and tidy - I could smell the man as he bent over to do up the bags, he was never sweet scented like Annie. More swearing occurred when he went into the bathroom and came back with a towel wrapped round his belongings, and he had to carry the bags and rolled-up towel downstairs to find another bag for that and his shoes and coat from the hall cupboard. As he stepped on to the top stair I bounded off the bed and followed him - he turned and I stopped and sat down quietly watching him, he almost tripped but just saved himself and with more loud and angry words continued down. That was when I had my great idea, and I slipped out of my little door in the kitchen as he began turning his shoes out of the cupboard and throwing them into a box he had found, adding the coat on top.

Outside the air was fresh with the scent of grass and flowers, reminding me of my lovely Annie. I hid behind the lavender bushes as the man came out, banging the door shut behind him and opening the car boot to bundle his bags and box in, then he climbed into the driving seat as I silently leapt on to the car roof. When I heard the engine start and felt the car move forward I jumped on to the bonnet, turning quickly to spread my claws across the glass and hiss and snarl at the man. I heard a loud groan, felt the car jerk to a stop at the edge of the pavement and saw the man slump forward on to the steering wheel. Triumph flooded through me as I waited for the inevitable swearing and prepared to run for my life - but he was still for so long I became frightened, I had meant to startle him, nothing more - or had I meant more? I began to get worried, Annie would be home soon and it seemed something was very wrong with the man.

I slid off the bonnet on to the pavement, taking care not to go off the edge, this was a main road and Annie was always telling me to be careful. That was what had given me the idea, I thought I would block his view, frighten him because he had to be able to see clearly but that was all and now I knew instinctively that he was either very ill or dead; I began to mew plaintively and soon a neighbour who was passing stopped to pet me and almost immediately saw what was wrong. By the time Annie arrived the ambulance was pulling up, the neighbour had taken the situation in at a glance and done what was necessary. I was right, he was dead and I wound myself around Annie's legs, full of remorse. I hated the man, he hated me but Annie had loved him, she must have done or she would never have put up with him; loud, hairy, dirty as he was and he never made a secret of how he felt about me and Annie's devotion to me.

Annie picked me up, tears were in her eyes but she shook her head when they asked her if she wanted to go in the ambulance. She hugged me tighter and the neighbour told how I had stopped her for help, and I began to think that now I might get away with this, Annie would never know that I had frightened the man, no one would suspect a small black cat.

Annie refused the company offered by her neighbour and carried me into the house. She made tea but did not drink it, she fed me but I could not eat and went instead to sit on her lap. At last she spoke to me. 'My baby,' she said, that was one of her pet names for me; she had several. 'So he's gone, and I think he was leaving me anyway, I saw what was in the boot.' I purred loudly and rubbed against her hand. 'So he was leaving me,' she whispered and tears slid silently down her face. 'It is so sad, I did love him once, but he changed so much and I know he was hard with you. I told him once I loved you more than I loved anyone and he never forgot it you know.'

I don't know how long Annie and I sat in the chair, but it was very dark when I slid off her lap to go outside and I did not stay, teasing Annie as I usually did and refusing to come in until she tempted me with treats or milk. Instead I hurried back and she got up then, and locked all the doors and windows and we went to bed. She was quick in the bathroom, usually the man would ask her why she had been so long and she would look at him and smile and climb into bed leaving her sweet smell behind to drift over me as I followed on to the bed to cuddle down beside her as I did now.

Annie was restless in the night, she often knocked me off the bed when she turned, or got out in the early hours when she could not sleep. Tonight she stayed in bed but I saw her eyes glinting and I knew she was awake most of the night. When the daylight seeped through the curtain I scratched at the bed and Annie looked at me sorrowfully. I suppose you want feeding as usual,' was all she said, and I felt bad because I had caused her sorrow. She came downstairs and fed me, this time I ate greedily, I was very hungry and Annie did at least drink the tea she made this morning.

The phone rang and I heard Annie say, 'Yes. No and thank you.' Then she told me, 'It was his heart, he had a weak valve and somehow it burst. May have been some kind of a shock they say. Perhaps the effort of finally making the decision to leave - or maybe . . . ' Annie looked at me, her eyes widening by the minute and I knew then that she had guessed. I sank on to the floor, expecting anger, loud anger or more tears, expecting to be thrown out. But no, instead Annie smiled slowly at me. 'I know how he treated you my beauty, (another pet name) and I can't blame you. I don't know what you did but it will be our secret for ever.' Annie picked me up as she said this, carried me to the worktop and put me down while she opened the cupboard and then the fridge. 'I'm going to cook a real breakfast today, they say I can stay off work for a week, more if I need to so we can lay around, watch TV, listen to music, read and do whatever we like, just the two of us.' I purred louder than I had ever done and waited impatiently as Annie slid sausages and bacon into the grill pan, and I saw her washing mushrooms and tomatoes. I love mushrooms and I knew Annie would save me some. Now she went to the fridge to get milk for her second cup of tea and poured me some, lifting my bowl on to the worktop beside her. 'Just the two of us,' she said again and I inhaled deeply of her sweet scent and lapped my milk.

THE MYSTERY OF THE NOBLEWOMAN
Ray Fenech

Valletta, besides being the capital city of Malta is, as Sir Walter Scott described it, 'a splendid town quite like a dream'. The town is called after the man who made this dream come to reality, Grand Master Jean Parisot de la Valette. The city is built on Sceberras Hill, being an ideal site for a fortress. The city is full of palaces and indeed a treasure trove for people interested in history and art.

There is a particularly beautiful house in St Ursola Street with its characteristic hundreds of steps, which was the venue of a particular haunting way back during World War II. Two naval officers are said to have met a strange lady one night as they were making their way down to the harbour, after spending some time ashore. She was extremely beautiful - a typical brunette with huge compelling brown eyes no man could resist.

Actually the woman stopped them outside the city's main gate and asked for their assistance saying she had apparently locked herself outside her home. The house which she referred to was on the way down to the harbour, so the two officers found no objection in helping her. When they arrived near the house, she pointed to a window which was only partly closed. There wasn't a single living soul, and being wartime all was in pitch darkness.

The two men were almost inclined to suspect that there was something strange about this woman, but her voice was so cultured and spellbinding that they dismissed these thoughts. Then one of the young officers scrambled up to the window. As he went through the house to get to the front door, he couldn't help noticing the magnificence of the style and taste with which the rooms were richly furnished. He thought that the family of the mysterious woman must be extremely well off and possibly of noble origins.

As he opened the front door, the light from the moon revealed a spotless marble floor that shone like a mirror. The lady then invited them for a drink and after smoking a cigarette, the two officers were ready to take leave of the beautiful host. After they left, the two men couldn't stop thinking about the mysterious woman. Suddenly one of the officers realised that he had lost his cigarette case.

The next day he decided to try and retrieve the cigarette case so together with his friend he set out to seek the house where they had spent some very pleasant hours the previous night. Hardly could they ever have imagined that they were in for the shock of their lives.

To start with, when they arrived to what they thought was the house they had visited, they realised that the place was in ruins. The stone of the facade was all flaked with humidity and the doors and windows were in an even sorrier state. Confirming that the house must have been closed for quite some years, were the massive weeds and cobwebs which barred the doorway.

The window through which he had made his way the previous night was in fact ajar and again, it was extremely easy to make one's way inside. As he entered, he had to use his matches in order to be able to make his way through the darkness in search of his cigarette case.

This was the same house alright, but it was hardly recognisable. The corridors were littered with rubbish and broken furniture. When he opened the front door and the sunlight seeped through he noticed that their footprints were still there from the previous night. The cigarette case was on the sofa in the sitting room, where the naval officer had left it purposely the night before, to have an excuse to return to see the beautiful woman.

BURGLARY IN PROGRESS
Alan Potter

Amanda was pleased to be home. The drive from her parents' house had been a long one. The delay on the motorway had added to the journey time. As she had passed the scene of the crash she could not help wondering what had happened to the people in the overturned car. The three lanes of extremely slow-moving vehicles began to speed up once the accident scene was left behind.

Her neighbour saw Amanda park her car at the front of the house and brought Skippy, Amanda's liver and white spaniel, to be reunited with his mistress. The dog wagged its tail ferociously and the joy of reunion was there for all to see.
'Thanks, Liz,' Amanda called over her shoulder, 'see you tomorrow.'

Once inside the house, the first thing Amanda did, as always on returning home from a visit, was to switch the kettle on. The panacea of all ills and the refreshing brew would soon be offering homecoming comfort, as it invariably did.

'Bedtime, Skip,' said Amanda, and the obedient spaniel immediately went to its basket in front of the kitchen radiator. Curled almost into a ball the dog settled down for the night and Amanda began to yawn as she climbed the stairs. There would be no need for sleeping pills, neither would she be reading very much of her book tonight. Almost as she switched out the bedside lamp she fell into a deep sleep.

Amanda stirred. She was far from being restless but she was half-aware that something had altered the depth of her sleep. The disturbance, whatever it was, was insufficient to bring her to full wakefulness and unconsciously she pulled the sheets more tightly around her before settling down once more.

Skippy was not so ready to return to sleep. He knew too that something had disturbed him and a low growl emanated from his throat. The dog was unable to identify the noise but there was little doubt that he had heard something. He lay in his basket with ears pricked ready to pick up the slightest indication of something amiss. Again he barked but louder this time.

Upstairs Amanda heard the bark and immediately came to full consciousness. She listened intently but heard nothing more than Skippy's growl. Something was outside, of that she was certain. Jumping out of bed she crossed to the window which overlooked her garden at the rear of the house. The pale moonlight cast its eerie shadow across the garden but there was no movement to disturb the quietude of the night. Skippy continued his growling and Amanda knew that he would not settle until she had gone downstairs and reassured him.

Dragging a dressing gown around her shoulders Amanda went to the kitchen. As she opened the door Skippy leapt from his basket and wagged his tail.
'What is it Skip?'

The dog, in reply, went to the rear door and planted his nose at the minuscule gap at the foot of the door. His low throaty growl continued softly and was sufficient to convince Amanda that something was moving outside.
'Shush, Skip,' she said as she carefully pulled one of the curtains aside. Still she saw nothing. She stood still and listened intently, nothing.
'On your bed,' the command in Amanda's voice told Skippy that he had done his job and his mistress was now in control. He returned to the basket and Amanda returned to her bed. Still tired, sleep returned swiftly.

***

In the police control room the hectic activity of the late evening and early hours of the morning had tailed off. Mentally tired operators relaxed, for after such busy nights they knew that the quieter periods were to be savoured for there were precious few of them. The clock ticked its slow yet inexorable way towards the dawn.

***

Skippy cocked an ear once more. He left his basket and padded his way across the kitchen floor to the rear door again. His ears told him that someone was moving about where they should not be and he knew that his ears never lied. A sudden sound prompted him to bark; he was warning his mistress in the only way he knew.

Amanda Forrester was instantly awake. Skip's barking was louder this time and certainly had a more urgent edge to it. She knew, as did her dog, that something was wrong. With dressing gown in place once more, she descended to the kitchen. This time Skippy did not leave the rear door to greet her. Amanda went to her pet and fondled his ears reassuringly. Both felt safer somehow.

Crouched at the foot of the door with an arm around the spaniel Amanda waited and listened. At first she could hear nothing but the tension of the dog's body told her that Skippy could. Still nothing. A few minutes later she heard it. It was not immediately obvious what the sound was and the stillness of the night did little to help her. Then again. This time she did identify it; breaking wood.

In the garden was the shed and in the shed were the lawnmower and all her garden tools. It must be those which were the thieves were after. Had there not been a number of such burglaries at her neighbours' houses over the past few weeks? Perhaps it was her turn now.

Standing up Amanda reached out for the door handle but then stopped. The tools were expensive and would have to be replaced but was that not why she had taken out insurance? Burglar or not Amanda decided that discretion far outweighed valour and she decided on a peek through the curtains as being the safer option. She could still see nothing but she could now hear movement out there from the direction of the shed. Burglars! Keeping low Amanda made her way to the lounge and the telephone. She dialled.

***

In the near silent police control room some operators fought against sleep. One or two had already succumbed. A buzzer caused everyone's eyes to glance at the telephony screen hoping that the call was not for their area.

'Police emergency.'
'Hello. I think someone is trying to break in,' Amanda whispered as loudly as she dared.
'Break in where?'
'My shed.'

'No I mean where do you live!' The operator silently tutted at the stupidity of the public.

Amanda gave her address and was then told not to hang up because the line would appear to go dead. The operator said that she was asking for a car to be sent immediately.

'OK, I'm back with you now. A car is already on its way. Can you see or hear anything now?'

'Nothing at all at the moment.'

'What exactly did you see?'

'Well nothing actually. I only heard a noise.'

'And what did the noise sound like?'

'It sounded as though someone was breaking wood. My shed is wooden and there have been quite a lot of burglaries to sheds in our area lately.'

'So you saw nothing?'

'Well no.'

'The police officers coming to you have just reported that they are entering your street. They will be with you very, very soon.'

'Thank you. Goodbye.' Amanda replaced the receiver as she heard a vehicle stop in the road outside.

***

The police car stopped a few yards from Amanda's house. The officers made their way quickly and quietly to the side gate. Both stood and listened but could hear nothing. They signalled each to the other and one officer waited at the gate whilst the other went to the narrow footpath at the rear of the house should the culprit try to make good his escape by that route. With a whispered 'go' both officers entered the garden simultaneously. They met near the shed which was securely locked. An examination of the exterior of the shed showed nothing amiss. The process was repeated around the outside of the house with a similar result.

Whilst one officer reported their findings, or rather lack of them, to control, the other went to speak to Amanda. She was relieved to hear his report but Skippy was obviously still not happy, his growl conveyed that clearly. The officers and Amanda, much braver now, went out to the garden and looked around as best they could with powerful torches cutting wide arcs of light into the darkness. The shed was indeed untouched.

'Well Miss Forrester,' said the senior of the two officers, 'as you can see, it doesn't look as though your shed's been attacked. Perhaps the dog disturbed who ever it was. There's certainly no sign of anyone out there now. Goodnight.'

'Goodnight and thank you.' Amanda waved a hand in thanks as the two officers returned to their car.

She went inside and decided that it was now too late to return to the warmth and comfort of her bed and after the excitement it was unlikely that she could sleep again.

Skippy returned to his basket and settled once more, his job was done.

Amanda switched the kettle on and soon afterwards sat at the kitchen table sipping slowly that hot but comforting first cup of tea of the day.

The badger left the garden through the rough hole in the lap fencing to return to its sett.

THE INSIDERS
Simon Halliday

The people of Grange Valley were more than ready for change. They had spent twenty-five years in the depths of poverty, with very little work. To look down on such a desperate situation would have filled the hardest heart with pity. The endless stream of hurt and anger had taken its toll on all of the residents, and none were more aware of this than Roman. A short and scrawny young man with no ambition, Roman had lived on dole money since escaping from his hated school five years ago. His only love was reading fiction, and somehow the recent aimless years had brought a curiosity he never expected, never fully realised - until the appearance of Paul Grey.

'The seat - is it taken?' Mr Grey had asked. Roman looked up as if emerging from a long sleep, then shook his head vaguely. The bus from town was damp and smelly. Large parts of the seats were ripped out, graffiti and dry vomit coloured the windows and floor. A woman shouted at her dog, and threw it off the seat as it began to urinate without a thought.

'Paul Grey,' said the stranger, sitting and putting a leather briefcase down very close to himself.

'Huh?'

'Paul Grey. What is your name?' The man extended a hand towards Roman, who eyed him with suspicion and mistrust.

'Who wants to know?' he managed, secretly feeling a vague recognition of this man.

'Simply being friendly,' said Paul openly, 'I just like meeting people. Who do you think I'm with - the men in black or something?'

It was perfectly delivered, and drew Roman in as planned. A mention of the police or local authorities would have clammed him up for good. Instead Roman laughed a little at the humour, but would not shake his hand. He was not good with people.

'Roman - Roman Kay.'

'I like it - very unusual,' said Paul. 'Women must find it fascinating, no?' He winked at Roman carefully, who smiled politely then turned away. 'Just pulling your leg,' continued Paul, 'don't take it so hard.'

'What do you want?' asked Roman, getting wise to the fact that there was more to this man than meets the eye. In the short gap in conversation that followed, the bus began to slow. The woman went to retrieve her dog, which was busy harassing a young couple. Paul's unusual eyes met Roman's and Roman could feel the urgency.

'This is our stop,' said Paul plainly, 'if you're in' The tired old brakes crunched the bus to a halt. Paul picked up his briefcase, stood up and walked off, brushing clean the sleeves of his expensive suit.

In what? was on Roman's lips, but he was given no time at all. Impulsively he ran after the man, tripping over the dog in his hurry. The dog yelped and the elderly woman scorned, but this was nothing to Roman's newly energised mind. None of that mattered right now, because something was definitely happening in his life.

'The world is cruel,' said Paul, 'to those who love it.' As the bus drew away, he stopped walking and Roman nearly ran into him in his hurry to keep up. They were in a quiet residential area, a place which Roman had often felt attracted to as he passed it on his way to town. Through the greasy bus windows, perhaps something about the tidy streets and healthy trees had been drawing his attention. The air seemed clear and there was a feeling of safety - protection even, which grew stronger now he'd got off the tiresome bus. Paul glanced around casually then headed towards a large, beautiful house.

As Roman followed, along the gravel path, he noticed delightful wild flowers and birds. Radiant colours and strikingly clear birdsong flooded his senses as Paul began to talk.

'Do you know the best thing about living in this valley?' asked Paul. He took a large bunch of keys from his inside pocket and opened the door. Paul answered his own question almost immediately, containing his enthusiasm in a low whisper as he shut the front door behind them - 'There are people like me in it.' Roman was no great moralist, but he immediately sensed the danger in this man's potential. Alarm bells were ringing, and not just metaphorically. He felt certain his ears were actually beginning to ring, an experience completely new to this young and inexperienced soul. There came a sense of fear, but the excitement remained. He glanced around at the enormous open hallway in which they stood. Polished mahogany floorboards, tasteful fine art and large houseplants. An open wooden staircase seemed to climb forever, in an overwhelming first impression to Roman's excited imagination.

'What . . .' began Roman, but he could not yet question this man. His head spun. Paul laughed in empathy.

'Come, let's get a drink, ' he said kindly. Roman followed him through a long but narrow section of the hallway, and felt he was stepping back in time. The surrounding decor was Victorian, but this was nothing to what he was being led into. They arrived in a great hall that had lots of seats, a lavish high ceiling . . and a stage - a beautiful theatre! Striking velvet curtains caught Roman's eye, and he wondered what lay behind. He had never been to the theatre, and previously had no idea that the pictures on television and magazines were so misleading. This place had *atmosphere*.

'Come on,' called Paul with a smile, 'the bar's this way.'

As the pair sat down a barman approached, looking distinctly Victorian in appearance. Paul ordered a glass of wine, and Roman asked for the same. He had a warm feeling that this drink would be unlike any other. It would be enjoyed in luxury, without raucous laughter and a need for excess. This was the beginning of a new adventure, maybe the start of a meaning for his life - a *place* for him. He looked around, wondering if he was in a dream or just losing his mind. The whole place was completely empty but for the two of them and the quietly spoken barman. Roman realised how eerie the situation had become, for now was also the moment of truth when he might get some answers to why this was happening. Paul was waiting for Roman to show some initiative, and in time Roman at last found his voice.

'Why have you brought me here?' he asked, startled at the echo around the high ceiling and walls.

'We can't do this any other way,' Paul began, 'it's the ignorance of the majority that allows our circle to grow in power.' He was analysing Roman's reaction in detail. The words seemed finely tuned and well rehearsed, and somehow Roman realised this. He became very suspicious, and looked through narrow eyes at Paul to show he was nobody's fool. Yet the confidence and coolness of the man was unshakeable, and Roman realised he would only learn what he was allowed to. To catch out or see through this man were not available options. Questions were the only key.

'What circle?' he asked, feeling a sensation as of walking towards an enormous mystical door. It was his choice alone as he began to knock, and he alone would experience the consequences. Paul's eyes were more penetrating than ever, and Roman felt his entire life pale into insignificance in this moment. Memories of past experiences flashed through his mind, in a surprising and terrifying review. Paul was drawing them out, as he considered Roman for whatever he had in mind.

'Interesting,' said Paul, 'very interesting.' He nodded thoughtfully then laughed in amusement.

'What?' asked Roman, 'what's funny?'

'You really should lighten up, you know' replied Paul, 'there's more to life than taking it seriously all the time.' The puzzle was beginning to annoy Roman, and he was annoyed for feeling this way.

'Can't you talk straight?' he demanded, 'Why all the cryptic riddles and clues?'

'Because' began Paul, smiling with playfulness, 'nothing is straight, and the whole of life is a cryptic riddle.'

As the barman arrived with the drinks, the words echoed around Roman's mind, - *the whole of life is a cryptic riddle*. What on earth was this man talking about? Roman had always been a quiet, introverted character. He had never been attracted to another human being in any way. He had no feelings for family or friends. He had lived his entire life inside his head, and had never understood that the things he read about in books really happened.

'What do you mean?' he asked, beginning to understand the extent of his naivety. Again Paul laughed, but Roman did not mind this any longer. He realised he might learn something if his patience held out for long enough.

'One day' began the answer, 'you will understand all of this, but for now we will watch a show. Bring your drink.'

Roman was led back to the theatre, and the two of them sat in the midst of hundreds of empty seats. Just then the lights dimmed and the curtains rolled open. A smoke machine was in full effect, and a green light created a wonderful feeling of mystery. Wondering whether he could take much more excitement for one day, Roman stared as three great mechanical monsters emerged from the smoke. The noise was tremendous - harsh metallic sounds as the machines made their way to the front of the stage.

'We can see you' came the grating voice. 'We are watching your every move, Roman Kay, so be very careful.'

The show was not to Roman's liking.

'What do they mean?' gasped Paul in horror, suddenly presuming this man was on his side in the face of such a display of power.

'Just a precautionary measure' said Paul lightly. 'You need to know who your friends are in this game.' At last Roman snapped, shouting at Paul.

'What game?' he demanded, 'is that all this is, a pathetic game of some bored, rich old eccentric? All this fancy display and crazy talk. What does it mean?' The machines continued to come, large crane-like constructions with bright headlights and caterpillar tracks. They crushed the front-row seats as they approached the two audience members. It was too much, and Roman ran away - out of the theatre and down the narrow corridor. His heart was racing as he hesitated to choose the right door, for the hallway had many. He chose the largest, praying he would emerge on the street.

As Roman opened the door the heads turned. A circle of eyes of thirty or so men was on him, and he simply wanted to wake up.

'Ah' said the man who was standing, 'here he is now.' The others just stared from their seats at the round table, and then it struck Roman that they all looked exactly the same as Paul. *Exactly.*

'Your time has come, my friend,' said the spokesman, who approached the young man with a gentle kindness. 'Your place awaits.' A memory suddenly came to Roman in a shocking realisation. The dream, the recurring dream he had in childhood. It was an image he had once wished for himself, a harmless fantasy, escapism from his ugly existence. As the associated blissful feelings rushed through Roman's senses, the man led him into a small room and sat him down. No resistance could be found as the body was slowly strapped down and the technology commenced its work.

DEPLOYMENT
Benjamin F Jones

The game began, if you could call it a game late one Friday night. Perhaps if I was being pedantic I would say it started a few months ago when I first noticed my neighbour thumping down the stairs to wake me; regular as clockwork at 04:12.

I asked her politely at first if she could keep the noise down a little, especially in the early hours. The request did nothing to reduce the volume whatsoever; if anything the situation got worse - she slammed doors harder in the communal hallway and played her music louder until later.

These opening gestures were just the flexing of muscles; the first moves in a game of chess before the heavy pieces come into play.

She is ready to go clubbing. Her music stops abruptly and she thuds down the stairs to slam the front door and climb into a taxi.

A brief pause
as in battle
itching and silent.

The house is a Victorian conversion, done quite recently on a very tight budget. I know very little about the landlord, except that he has a couple of dogs that often eat the rent cheques; we then have to write him another at the request of his panicky letters. Our floor of the house is bisected by a narrow carpeted hallway which runs from the front door and along to a rear where it overlooks a meagre garden; I believe I have the key to this door but as yet I have seen no reason to set foot on the wasteland tip.

I prop open the door between my flat and the communal hallway with a copy of the yellow pages and unscrew the cap of the chlorpyrifos. As I give a liberal soaking to the threshold of my abode and the area directly beyond it, the characteristic smell curdles with that of hairspray and perfume from the flat opposite.

I work in a laboratory just out of town so these things are easy to get hold of; I breed drosophila and other small insects. So my company also supplied the glassware, filters and fixtures that make up the other part of my retaliation; a double ended glass bulb with an exit bore to be connected to a pipe but currently blocked with bung, and an entry coupling complete with gauze filter and one-way valve to be connected to a bicycle pump.

Pulling a length of silicone tubing from my bag, I began to feed the pipe into the gap beneath my neighbour's door, rather like performing an endoscopy. Once this process was complete I tipped up the vessel and removed the bung, quickly pushing the tubing onto the exposed coupling.

The fleas jumped in their vessel as they felt the warmth of blood through the fragile glass; 47 grams of insane black siphonaptera, starved and ready for action.

An experimental push on the bicycle pump sent the first squadron of macroscopic knights pouring down the tube; an ejaculation of irritation, rattling into my enemy's fortress. I pumped carefully and steadily until the last of my soldiers was deployed.

In the silence that followed I could hear them bouncing expectantly at objects in the untidy room as they waited for her return.

A CHRISTMAS RESOLUTION
Tina Foster

I stood on the hillside gazing out over the snow-covered landscape. Everywhere was white except for odd hints of green from the pine trees spread out in clusters over the hillsides. It was a beautiful sight which I looked at every year, if the snow fell, from when I was young and small until now older and bigger. Can any other place be like this, birds, wildlife and peace?

Now I am in the comfort of a warm, well-decorated and light livingroom. The family are all busy preparing for the Christmas celebration gathering, Mum in the kitchen, Dad building up the fire and the two young boys were running about in excitement at their pleasure of seeing me. As for the young girl, huddled up in an armchair, she was deep in thought, she has only glanced at me once or twice but I saw no pleasure in her eyes at seeing me. Not uttering a word to anyone. Auntie was being her usual annoying self trying to organise everyone and waving a finger of disapproval at me but I tried to become oblivious to her and could not understand what she was annoyed about. I could see that she was causing upset and disarray to everyone.

At bedtimes I had time alone to gaze at the cosiness of the room but the well-lit fire burning piled with logs caused me sadness. It was warm and comfortable though. The excitement went on for days and I was always contributing my part. One evening Mum and Dad spent wrapping presents piles and piles of them as I watched.

All at once Christmas Day was upon us. I was caught up in the excitement of it all. Paper was discarded everywhere as presents were unwrapped, everyone was happy, so was I. Would I be able to stay here for the rest of my days with them all, watching them all in this comfort. I did not feel good though, had not felt good for days. Felt droopy and lifeless all over. No one seemed to notice though that I was not as I should be.

Days passed and all at once Mum and Auntie were removing the cards and Auntie was saying over and over again 'how glad she was it was all over until next year'. What was over? Now she turned to me and began removing the decorations from my branches. What was happening? I was already shedding my needles and my branches were becoming bare, were the decorations causing it, was this why I did not feel as I should? With a couple of wrenches I was removed from my pot of earth and was being pushed harshly through the door. The cold air hit me and I felt the climate change from warm to cold. Suddenly I was thrown in the air and landed harshly upon a pile of dead vegetation. I was dying, why, like others of my kind my time of glory, of being admired was over, how long had it lasted some two to three weeks. Why could I not be on the hillside again looking at the scenery with all the others of my kind, pines who probably next year may have the same Christmas adventure and then fate that I had had after years of growth. Surely there must have been an alternative to removing us from the hillside to play such a short, small part, of being admired and then forgotten. Could something else not have been used in my place?

Some miles away in a small newsagents was a sign which read:
'Let the natural pine trees flourish, buy an artificial one'.

TALES OF ALEISHA
Jean Rhodes

Aleisha aged three and three quarters, because it was nearly autumn when she would be four, was examining the dahlias in the herbaceous border. She had just come home, and was neat and tidy. Her long blonde hair was tied up in a ponytail with a nice shiny green ribbon.

'What are you looking at?' I asked, weeding the rockery with dogged determination - I *hate* weeding.

'There's something in here.'

'For Heaven's sake - what?'

There was a faint scream from Aleisha who did a quick back somersault from the bright yellow dahlia she had been studying. I got up swiftly, banged my head on a branch, winced and rushed over.

'What is it?'

'Ugh.'

'Well?'

'There's a nasty brown thing in there - with horns.'

'Eh?' I looked more closely.

A large brown earwig looked back at me.

'It's an earwig' I said picking Aleisha up and dusting her down. 'Earwigs are very good mothers. She is probably looking for something to feed her babies on.'

'She doesn't *look* very nice' said Aleisha, unconvinced by my argument on earwig mothers. 'My mother is pretty.'

I sat down in the grass and thought this one over. It is true to say, that to humans, earwigs are definitely *not* pretty.

'Come here' I said.

'What?'

'Well - let's think about this - you are not an earwig.'

'Ugh - there's another one here and they all look alike - ugly.'

'OK. Let's look at it from the earwig's point of view. Perhaps they think that all humans look alike and are ugly, and perhaps, like humans, some earwigs are prettier than others.'

'Mmm' Aleisha thought about this for a while. 'P'raps we don't look nice to earwigs at all.'

'Well that might be true. After all - all we do is scream at them and say - ugh what horrible things, you never know, they *might* be saying exactly the same thing about us.'

'As well as thinking we are giants' said Aleisha, obviously warming to the theme.

'Well, yes.'

'Why are earwigs good mothers?'

'Let's see.'

The earwig was descending the dahlia stalk, waving her head and obviously watching us for danger signals. We sat very still in the grass and watched.

'Of course they will be nearly grown up by now' I whispered to Aleisha who was very concerned about how the earwig would make the big drop to the ground from the lower leaves of the dahlia without hurting herself.

'Shush.'

The earwig suddenly let go, opened her pathetic wing guards for a fleeting second and dropped without harm into the herbaceous border.

'I didn't know they had wings' said Aleisha turning to me in astonishment.

'Well, they don't use them much, only as a sort of parachute.'

I then had to spend quite a while explaining the principles of parachuting. Every so often, I forgot that nearly four-year-olds need simple explanations!

'Whoops' said Aleisha who had caught up with the earwig again. 'Where is she going now?'

The mother earwig was making for a little patch of garden alongside the now defunct peonies. As we watched and *really* looked we could see a little hole leading into a pile of dead leaves.

Our vision seemed to have improved, because at the entrance to the hole we could see three lots of little brown horns appearing as the mother approached.

'I want to go too' said Aleisha.

'You are far too big.'

The mother earwig on the brink of her nest, suddenly turned and fixed me with a beady earwig eye.

'No she isn't,' she said in a squeaky little voice. 'Do her good - teach her a thing or two.'

Aleisha disappeared.

As I gazed anxiously at the hole, I could only tell her from the other earwigs because she had a bright green ribbon waving about her antenna. She waved this at me cheerfully and disappeared down the hole with the mother earwig gently shepherding her in.

Suddenly our garden thrush 'Tom Thrush' appeared, and made a beeline for the hole down which they had all vanished. I am very fond of Tom, but the thought of Aleisha being gobbled up as well as all the rest of the family put me into a panic.

'Go away Tom' I shouted at him.

He looked mortally offended and flew off in a huff.

After what seemed like hours, a small brown earwig with a bright green ribbon, emerged from the hole.

Mother earwig anxiously followed gazing carefully around before allowing this foster baby to emerge completely.

I bent down to catch what she was saying.

'You must *always* have somewhere to hide. Never stay in the open too long or the birds will get you. Stay low to the ground and don't make yourself too obvious.' She eyed the green ribbon with disfavour. 'If you are going to be a real earwig, I should get rid of that! Now be careful and remember what I've said.'

The small brown earwig with the green ribbon turned round and linked antennae for a moment with the older female. 'Thank you' it said. 'I've had a lovely time and the food was brill. I'm sorry I won't see Abe, Jack, Sue, Gerry, Mary, Alison, Picky or Fred anymore, but I have to go back. Jean is waiting for me and she'll be worried.'

'I understand' said the mother earwig. 'Just do as I've told you and take care. Oh, and try to stop that woman of yours from digging everywhere so vigorously. She should make sure there are no earwig nests around first.'

'I'll try,' said Aleisha 'but she is a very enthusiastic digger.'

I was still sitting in the grass.

I could see the little earwig coming towards me with its green ribbon waving. As it reached my leg there was a funny noise, and there was Aleisha. Her hair ribbon was undone, and she looked pretty untidy.

'What *have* you done to your hair?' I asked, retying the ribbon and making her look reasonably respectable.

'Well' said Aleisha. 'Abe, Sue, Gerry, Mary, Alison, Jack, Picky and Fred thought it was a great game to play with it, so I got a bit untidy.'

'A bit! Tell me about the family?'

'Oh it's a super family. The nest is lovely and clean and there's always plenty of food. Nice rotted vegetables and tasty little grubs. Mmm, lovely.'

'Did you eat some of that?' I asked rather gobsmacked.

'Of course.'

'Oh well, every earwig to its own.'

Aleisha suddenly realised what she had said.

'I feel sick!'

'Well, at least you made a lot of new friends.'

'Oh yes, they were lovely, and such fun to play with.'

'I suppose,' I said 'that you will be keen to protect these earwigs from now on?'

Aleisha ran around the back of the house and came back with two bamboo canes. 'Here,' she said, 'put these in to mark the nest, and *do* be careful where you dig in future.'

'Yes' I said meekly and followed her home.